Still the One

HARPER BLISS

Still the One

Copyright © 2023 by Harper Bliss

Published by Ladylit Publishing – an imprint of First Page V.O.F., Belgium

ISBN-13 9789464339284

D/2023/15201/02

Edited by Cheyenne Blue

Proofread by Claire Jarrett

Cover design by Caroline Manchoulas

CHAPTER 1

Mac

There she is. The woman who broke my heart into a million pieces. Jamie Sullivan, owner of Sully's Sourdough—and cheater extraordinaire.

I've had months to prepare for this moment—years even—but maybe there's no such thing as preparing for something like this.

I'm definitely not ready for how untouched by time she looks. Her hair is still that rich dark brown—surely this can't be her natural color anymore—and she's still sporting those same bangs that almost hide her eyes.

Jamie makes a beeline for me. "Wow. Gabrielle Mackenzie in the flesh." She flashes me a smile. "I see you on TV all the time, but…" She pauses, looks me in the eye briefly before her glance skitters away. Jamie shakes her head ever so slightly, then asks, "Can I give you a hug?"

"Yeah." I inhale deeply. It's been twenty years. I've had to move on with my life and in order to do so, I had to forgive Jamie for what she did—for ripping my heart to shreds—but I will never forget. It's not possible. "Sure." I open my arms for what I think will be a light embrace—

keeping each other at a respectable distance while gingerly folding our arms around each other. But Jamie has other plans—that's kind of her thing.

She pulls me close. I have no choice but to bury my nose in that gloriously soft hair of hers. It feels like silk and smells like the most fragrant flowers.

"Sandra and her adult-onset heteronormativity, eh?" Jamie says, her mouth right by my ear.

"My thoughts exactly." We let go, and I have no time to investigate my feelings, no time to gauge if there's anything left at all of what I used to feel for Jamie, because Sandra, the reason we're both here, bounds up to us.

"Good," Sandra says, pointing her finger from me to Jamie. "This has happened. It's done." She narrows her eyes. "I'm smart enough not to ask how that made you feel. For once, it's all about me." She waggles her eyebrows. Poor Sandra. She's been in the middle of our feud since the very beginning. No wonder she asked—demanded, really—that we finally get over ourselves so we could both attend her dream wedding in Maui. And here we are.

"It *is* all about you, gorgeous." Jamie rubs Sandra's shoulder. She's still as tactile as ever, then. "Where do you want us? What should we do?"

We? Wow. That was quick. Still bossy then, as well. Or, as Jamie used to call it: taking charge of a situation.

"That lovely man over there"—Sandra points to the wedding planner I met when I arrived earlier today—"is going to tell you all about it. This is only the rehearsal so if you'd like to practice sitting together, that can be arranged." She throws in a wink.

"There's no assigned seating?" Jamie sounds incredulous.

"Just sit on my side of the aisle," Sandra says. "And be nice to each other. That's all I want." She pulls her lips into the widest grin. "Thank you both for being here. It means a lot that you've put aside your, um, differences. For me."

Perhaps I should have done that a long time ago, for the numerous parties of Sandra's that I missed because I feared Jamie might be there. But so many things that shouldn't happen, do—to remind myself of that I only have to glance at the woman standing next to me. And I had to say yes to Sandra's wedding.

"The best excuse ever for a trip to Hawaii," Jamie says in that way she has. It should sound obnoxious—because we're not here for an exotic holiday; we're here for our friend—but for some reason that has always eluded me, it doesn't. Jamie gets away with everything. "It's an honor to be here," Jamie continues. "But I'm not going to lie, San, I'm still a little baffled at you tying the knot. Life can be funny that way."

"The heart wants what the heart wants," is all Sandra says, before she's whisked off by the wedding planner.

"So?" Jamie tilts her head. "Do you want to sit with me?"

"Why not?" My smile is surprisingly genuine. Maybe instead of being cut up about seeing my ex-fiancée again, I'm simply glad to spend some time with my former best friend. It must be that.

"Come on." Jamie leads the way to where we're meant to sit. It gives me a chance to thoroughly scrutinize her from behind. She's dressed in a soft pink suit and her ass looks mighty fine in those pants.

We find a spot in the middle row of only three. This is

not a huge wedding, just the bride and groom's immediate families and a small number of friends.

"Oh! My! God!" a high-pitched voice comes from behind us. "Hell has finally frozen over. What's next? Flying pigs?"

Jamie and I turn around. Alan stares back at us. He's one of the friends I gradually lost after Jamie and I broke up—someone who, over time, gravitated more toward her. I don't hold it against him. I spend a lot of time abroad and when in New York, I'm usually busy with work.

"Hi, darling." We both stand up and Jamie air kisses him.

"My god, Mac! As I live and barely fucking breathe." Alan holds out his hands. Instinctively, I put mine in his. "Phew. You look even hotter than you do on TV. Positively smoking, darling. Hot damn, it's so good to see you. Come here." He pulls me to him and the enthusiastic kisses he plants on my cheeks have nothing airy about them.

"It's wonderful to see you, Alan." The tight-knit group of friends Jamie and I were part of brusquely fell apart after she left me. In the end, Sandra was the only one I kept in close contact with. "You look smoking hot as well, Alan." I rake my gaze over my old pal. He's still the same man I used to see all the time, except his hairline has receded and his face looks more weathered. I used to know every intimate detail about Alan's life and now here we are, not quite strangers, but certainly no longer friends.

"Babe, come here." Alan calls for a man a few feet away with his back to us. He turns around and joins us. "Please meet my far better half. This is Charles." Alan wiggles his fingers to draw attention to the ring on his ring finger. "My husband." Alan beams when he says the word. Another wedding I wasn't invited to. I wonder how many there have been. Am I the only single person here? Jamie might not have brought a plus-one, but I doubt someone like her is single—unless that's how she wants it. Although, come to think of it, people always say that about me as well. As though having my face on TV automatically makes me prime relationship material. But there are a million reasons to remain single. I should know—so I shouldn't judge.

Charles is dashing, well-spoken, and extremely courteous. I wonder how he ended up with the likes of Alan, who is foul-mouthed, outrageous, and says whatever he thinks no matter whose company he's in.

"Can we sit with you, Mac?" Charles asks, surprising me. Mac is what my friends call me, and I've only just met him. It could still be what Alan calls me when he sees me on TV. "I'm such a fan of—"

"Babe." Alan leans into Charles's ear and tries to whisper—but being inconspicuous has never been one of Alan's talents. "Give them some space," he says.

"It's all right," I say. "We don't need space." Why would Jamie and I need space? We're not here for a reunion; we're here for our friend's wedding.

"Nevertheless." Did Alan just wink at me? "We'll see you at the rehearsal dinner. We're sitting at the same table." He drags Charles away, but they can't sit very far from us.

"Don't mind Alan," Jamie says. "You know he always has silly notions."

"Like what?" Jamie and I sit again and I take a good look at her face. She has aged, of course, but time has been kinder to her than it was to Alan. She's still as stunning as when I first met her—better, even. Because those lines around her eyes promise the kind of wisdom no one has at twenty, or thirty for that matter. When they play reckless games with the heart of the person they're meant to love most in the world.

"Let's just say he has made rather a big deal of you being here."

"Why?"

Jamie pulls her lips into a grin. "Come on, Mac. Surely, you know why."

"Because we haven't seen each other in twenty years."

"Well, yes, although that's not technically true. We did see each other—"

"Is Alan expecting some big drama or something?" I cut Jamie off for a reason. I don't want to relive the couple of excruciating times I ran into her, or arrived somewhere I thought she wouldn't be only to be confronted with her when I was nowhere near ready for that. "Because too much time has gone by for that."

"That's exactly what I said to him."

"Charles seems lovely."

"He's such a gem."

"How long have they been married?"

"Coming up to seven years now." Something sparkles in Jamie's eyes. I remember that sudden glint in her eyes well. It was one of the things that made her irresistible— that made me fall in love with her over and over again. "Guess who officiated their nuptials?"

The way she's looking at me, there can only be one answer. "You?"

"I got ordained as a Dudeist Minister. Isn't that the most hilarious thing you've ever heard? Me? Officiating for The Church of Dudeism." Jamie sure thinks it's a hoot. "Marrying two dudes."

It is funny, though. Jamie's laughter is infectious—

always has been. It's a little awkward to be sitting here with her, after all these years, but despite everything that has happened, there's something familiar, something strangely soothing about it as well. For ten years of my life, I had the privilege of knowing Jamie Sullivan in the most intimate ways. Maybe it says a lot about me that, in hindsight, they were the best years of my life.

"It's such a Jamie thing to do," I say when our chuckles die down.

"Hey, um, I've been nervous about seeing you again." Jamie's face has turned all serious. "When you first started appearing on TV, I had to switch it off, and you know how much I love watching sports." She scoffs softly, as though mocking herself. "But I'm glad you came. That you're here."

"I'm here for Sandra."

"Yeah. We all are."

The seats around us suddenly fill up, as though the wedding planner just flipped a switch. We are hushed so the rehearsal can start—and my first proper conversation with Jamie in twenty long years is cut short.

CHAPTER 2

Jamie

"To America." Alan lifts his champagne glass. "Where we're so uptight, we feel the need to practice for the best day of our life." He rolls his eyes. "They don't do that anywhere else in the world, you know?" He shoots his husband a wink. "Charles and I were very un-American about it. We skipped the rehearsal and went straight for the wedding instead."

"You're very worldly like that, darling," I say, and my poor brain can't help it. Attending this wedding and being here with Mac takes me back to the time she and I were planning our own commitment ceremony—back in the dark ages before same-sex marriage was legal. We had it all figured out—all the various steps meticulously mapped out. Until Cherry came along.

"The rehearsal dinner is more an opportunity for the two families to come together," Mac says, using her sexy broadcaster voice. It makes her sound as though she possesses all the wisdom in the world. "Because our country is so big, we tend to marry more outside of our immediate circle than in other places."

"I'd never looked at it like that." Charles gazes at Mac like a genuine fanboy would. Who can blame him? Mac is a spectacular woman. She still has the slim, fit body of the soccer player she used to be. Her satin-like blonde hair just touches her shoulders. Her bright blue eyes stand out. Her complexion is radiant. And that sleeveless blouse is showing off some serious muscle definition.

We used to hold our very own arm-wrestling competitions—the baker against the former athlete. Kneading-dough strength versus gym-built strength. Mac always won. Losing isn't really her thing.

"Hello friends." Sandra crouches next to us at our table of four. "Everything going okay?" She eyes me first, then Mac.

"Hunky-dory," Alan says.

"Mac, I'm so sorry, but my father-in-law is absolutely dying to meet you. Could you just give him a quick hello so he can get on with his life?"

"Sure." Mac doesn't seem perturbed by this. Her rise to TV fame happened after we broke up. When we were together, she was still working behind the scenes. I watch her rise and follow Sandra to the family table.

"How are you feeling?" Alan asks when Mac is out of earshot.

Before I can reply, he continues. "What's it like seeing her again?"

I huff out some air. "It's a little overwhelming. She's so—"

"Classy? Elegant? Charming? Hot?" Alan's on a roll.

"Absolutely gorgeous and so down-to-earth," Charles adds.

"Wow." I arch up my eyebrows. "Are you both crushing on Mac now?"

"Is she single? What do you know?" Alan doesn't even acknowledge my question.

"As much as you do."

"I follow her on Instagram," Charles says, "and there's never any mention of a partner or anything like that, although that doesn't necessarily mean anything."

"Surely Sandra knows," Alan says. "They must still be pretty tight for Mac to come all the way to Maui for her wedding." He taps his chin, as if we haven't known for months that Mac would be here. But for the longest time, it was just an abstract notion in the future. Now the moment is here and we're sharing a table with her. Mac has become very real for us—for me—again and, no matter how I twist or turn it, it's a shock to my system.

"Don't worry, *James*," Alan says, calling me by his special nickname for me. "I'm on it. By the end of this night, I'll know all there is to know about Mac's personal life." He sighs. "I can only speak for myself, but it's so good to see her again. It's been way too long."

"What do you want to know?" Mac puts her hands on Alan's shoulders and stands there beaming a smile at us. We were so wrapped up in talking about her, we stopped paying attention to where she was.

"We're curious about you." Alan isn't fazed by Mac overhearing him—indiscretion is his middle name and surely Mac must remember what he's like. "It's only normal."

Mac gives Alan's shoulders a squeeze and takes her seat again. "In that case, let's go tit for tat."

"I'd prefer if no tits were involved." Alan pulls a horrified face.

Mac shakes her head at him, then turns to me with a look that says 'Can you believe this guy?'

11

I can only respond with a shrug. Alan's been one of my best friends for most of my life. But maybe Mac needs to reacclimatize to him a little.

"But sure," Alan says. Although I appreciate his company and the levity it brings, I'd love to ask Mac a couple of questions in private. "Ask us anything you want, Mac."

Instead of asking Alan a question, Mac turns to me. For a split second, I fear she might ask me how things turned out with Cherry, right here in front of my friends. But that's not Mac's style.

"Are you single?" she asks.

"Booyah!" Alan mimics an explosion with his fingers.

"I am," I answer truthfully. "You?" The question naturally flows from my lips.

Mac nods.

"I don't think we're going to have to answer a lot of questions, babe," Alan says to Charles. "We can just sit back and enjoy the lezzie show." He crosses his arms over his chest, probably a little offended at not being the center of attention, and leans back.

I'm dying to inquire further, to ask Mac about her love life after me. Sandra refused to discuss that with me, claiming that if I wanted to know, I should find an adequate way to apologize to Mac so we could be friends again, and she could tell me herself. But Mac made it crystal clear she never wanted anything to do with me ever again—and that served me right.

"You must have so many admirers," Charles says, sounding baffled at Mac's admission.

Mac just shakes her head. She never fully grasped how beautiful she is. Although being on TV must earn her many compliments about her looks.

"Is it true there's a special Tinder for celebrities?" Try as he might, Alan can't keep quiet for longer than a few minutes.

To my surprise, Mac nods. I'm not surprised a dating app like that exists, but I am that Mac would use it. But it's just another reminder that I know nothing about her any longer—about the woman I was going to marry and start a family with.

"Aaah!" Alan coos. "Have you used it?"

Mac nods slowly. "I have, but… I'm sorry, darling. I'm not spilling any beans."

Alan clutches both hands to his chest. "Not even a tiny little bean?"

"I'm still single so clearly it wasn't that successful." Mac fixes her gaze on Alan. "But guess who's a regular at Isabel Adler's house?" She paints on a triumphant smirk, displaying a side of her that's either new or that I don't remember.

Alan's mouth falls open. "No!" He shouts it as though our table has just caught fire. The other guests stop their conversations to look at us. "You can tease me about anyone else in the world, but not about Isabel Adler. That woman is a goddess and we are but mere mortals worshipping at her feet."

Mac bursts out laughing and so do I. There's theatrics, and then there's this. I can't help but eye her inquisitively myself, though.

"I'm good friends with Leila, her partner," Mac says.

Alan looks at me with genuine devastation in his glance, as though he stayed friends with the wrong person after Mac and I broke up.

"She's my ex, actually," Mac continues.

"Isabel Adler's partner is your ex." Alan brings the back of his hand to his forehead, as though he might faint.

"Yeah, I can see that," Charles mumbles, gently nodding.

Can he? I've never been able to imagine Mac with anyone else. In fact, it's always been my greatest fear that I'd run into her on the arm of some gorgeous woman—no matter what kind of a hypocrite that would make me. Because I'm the one forever responsible for breaking us up. Although my guilt would be greatly alleviated if Mac were happily married, with the bunch of kids she always wanted—but still. But she must have had her fair share of lovers, of women adoring her—and not breaking her heart the way I did.

I tune back into the conversation just as Alan asks, "Forgive my indiscretion, darling." He looks Mac straight in the eye and his voice is firm and solemn, like he's taking Mac's confession and she has no choice but to answer him. Alan's specialty is extracting secrets from another person. "But why did things not work out between you and Leila Zadeh?"

Mac scoffs, or is that a giggle? "Let's just say I've had some issues with trusting people in my life."

That even shuts Alan up for a few moments. But thankfully not for too long. "It probably wasn't meant to be," he muses. "Because Leila was meant to be with Isabel."

"Why are *you* single?" Mac takes me completely by surprise with her question.

"Hm." I look into her eyes. Even though what she just said was an obvious—and deserved—dig at me, her face is kind and welcoming. "I haven't always been single. I'm just more of a serial monogamist, I guess," I blurt out.

14

"You most certainly are," she says. "Minus the monogamy."

"Zing!" Alan interjects, and I'm glad he does, because I don't know what to say to that. "Good one, Mac, darling, but, um, this is all water under the bridge now, isn't it?" He arches up his eyebrows. "Twenty years' worth of water."

"Of course," Mac says, nodding. "I'm sorry." She briefly touches her hand to my shoulder, startling me again. "I shouldn't have said that. Alan's right. It *is* water under the bridge."

"Please, Mac, don't apologize." I can only hope the smile I send her hides my guilt. I've had to let go to move on, but I've never had the chance to properly apologize to Mac. At the time, she didn't want my apologies—what could she do with some futile words, anyway? Then our worlds drifted farther and farther apart as the years went on. Now here we are, two decades later. "Don't ever apologize to me," I say.

CHAPTER 3

Mac

When I head into the hotel restaurant for breakfast the following morning, Charles accosts me.

"You're very welcome to sit with us, but I have to warn you Alan is completely losing it over you knowing Isabel Adler. Like, *totally*." He heaves a deep sigh. "He's forgotten all his good manners and he already had so few." Charles grins sheepishly.

I look over at the table where Alan's sitting. He's waving at me. There's no sign of Jamie.

"I think I can handle your husband," I say.

"When it comes to Isabel Adler, he's next-level intense. It's kind of endearing." Charles doesn't sound entirely convinced.

"I suppose I don't have to ask what the first dance song was at your wedding," I joke, giddy at the prospect of Alan hearing which song Sandra and Tyrone's first dance will be to.

Alan gets up to greet me and hugs me tightly. "I barely slept a wink because of the mere one degree of separation. *One.*" He holds up his finger. "One is not zero, but there are so many options."

"This is what I mean," Charles says. "He's lost it."

"Okay." I hold out my hands and Alan takes them. "What can I do to make you snap out of this? I can't have you going gaga over Izzy all weekend. It's crazy enough that I'm here with Jamie. I need you to defuse the tension between us."

"Tension?" Alan tilts his head. "What tension?" He isn't that far gone that he can't crack a joke any longer.

He squeezes my hands. "Can you get me in a room with Isabel Adler?"

"Babe," Charles groans. "It's too much. Besides, you wouldn't be able to handle it."

"Oh, I would. I would rise to that occasion like you have no idea." He focuses on me again. "How well do you know her? Do you see her a few times a year? Or do you and her actually hang out on the regular?"

"I'm more friends with Leila, but yeah, Izzy and I do hang out sometimes." I make a mental note to call Leila after breakfast. She'll want to know how my reunion with Jamie went. I might not tell her about this, though.

"I don't really know how to process this yet," Alan says on a sigh.

"Lucky you're stuck in this resort with two lesbians, then," I attempt another joke. "We're very good at processing."

"I'm not so sure about that, darling." Alan comes back to himself for a moment. "Last night, it looked to me as though you and Jamie have some serious processing left to do."

He's right—but he's also wrong. Maybe Jamie and I should have a conversation, but we can just as easily choose not to. Our lives won't be changed by it and I, for one, am no longer after some sort of closure. Some things might get said inadvertently—but isn't that always the case? What she did will always be a part of me, and I'm okay with that now.

"Back to Izzy." I look him in the eye.

"I know what I sound like, and, for the record, I am exactly that: the biggest Isabel Adler fan you will ever meet. I swear to god, Mac. I'd give anything to meet her."

"I'll see what I can do." I can't make this man I haven't spent time with in years any real promises.

"Thank you so much. That's all I ask. Like, maybe there's a dinner party you could invite us to now that we've become reacquainted? I'll cook. It would be my honor to cook for you and Leila and Isabel."

"He *is* an excellent cook," Charles deadpans.

"Maybe we can even invite Jamie," Alan says, as though this dinner is a done deal already. "How would you feel about that?"

"You're pushing it." I drop his hands from mine. "Jamie is… the past. I'm not looking to be friends with her or anything like that."

"How about two fabulous gays as old and new friends at the same time?" Alan bats his lashes.

"Let's see how the rest of this weekend goes," I only half-joke. Although it is lovely to see Alan, and to meet his husband. They're both delightful company—maybe Izzy and Leila would agree.

"Seriously, though, Mac." Charles pours me a glass of water. "How do *you* feel?"

"I don't know. It's a bit of a whirlwind." I take a sip. "I'm not going to lie. It is weird to see Jamie again, the woman I've purposefully avoided for so long. She was such a big part of my life." Outside of work, Jamie *was* my life. For a full decade, we spent all our free time together, basking in each other's company, and dreaming up an amazing joint future. I loved Jamie so much; she was a part of me. And when a part of yourself gets abruptly ripped away, it takes a long time to heal. "I can't pretend I didn't love the hell out of her, nor can I pretend that what happened between us didn't." I look around the room. "Where is she, anyway?"

"Probably sleeping in while she can," Alan says. "She's always up so early when she's working."

I nod as my mind travels back twenty-five years, to the loud blare of Jamie's alarm clock at an ungodly hour. To her apprenticeship with Loaves of Love, Brooklyn's most famous bakery, where she always seemed to have the early shift.

"Isn't she the big boss now?" I ask. "Doesn't that come with better hours?" I reach for a piece of bread in the basket on the table. When we lived together, Jamie always had bread on the go, a sourdough starter to tend to, some rolls to put into the oven. I've never met anyone since who could wax so lyrical about the crumb of a loaf.

"You would think so," is all Alan says.

"Are you and her still thick as thieves?" I look him in the eye. I might no longer hold it against Alan that he chose Jamie over me, that doesn't mean I haven't missed him.

"Oh, yes." He scrunches his lips into the infamous Alan pout. "I really tried to keep in touch with you, Mac, but… over time, it just didn't happen."

"He's been beating himself up over that so much as we approached this wedding." Charles lovingly pats his husband on the shoulder.

"It's okay." I was so angry for such a long time, I made myself pretty much unreachable by working all the time. My career soared; my private life not so much. "As you said last night, it's all water under the bridge now. Although seeing Jamie again is so…" I huff out some air. My gaze darts to the restaurant entrance and, as if I conjured her up by saying her name, there she is. Jamie's hair's messy and she's barely wearing any clothes apart from something long and baggy hanging off her shoulders.

Alan and Charles turn to follow my gaze. Charles gets up and ushers Jamie toward us.

"You look like you had a rough night," Alan says as he sends her a warm smile.

"Must be jet lag." Jamie pins her gaze on me briefly but glances away quickly, as though she can't look at me properly in the morning light. "I couldn't get to sleep until the early hours."

"Then jet lag must have a reverse effect on you." Alan eyes Jamie.

"You know I keep odd hours," Jamie says.

"Let's get you some coffee." Charles throws an arm around Jamie's shoulders and gives her a squeeze. He's such a sweet man.

"Thank you, darling." Jamie blows Charles a kiss while he pours her a cup of coffee, then she finally looks at me properly. "Turns out seeing you again is much more of a mind fuck than I had anticipated."

What am I supposed to say to that? I'm sorry? I don't think so—because I'm not. Because I didn't do anything wrong.

"Same." I glance at Jamie's exhausted face. She looks vulnerable. Shaken.

"Can we talk today? Before everything kicks off?" she asks. "Have a proper conversation?"

I guess it's inevitable, although the last thing I came here for was to open up old wounds—to pick at scar tissue that took forever to grow. Because I might not have known then, but Jamie did so much more than break my heart. She stole my biggest dream as well.

"Sure."

"After breakfast?" Jamie manages a small smile. "As soon as I've put myself together?"

"Okay." Why am I feeling sorry for her? The one emotion I vowed to myself I'd never associate with her ever again.

"Thank you." Her dark gaze lingers on mine for a moment before she takes a slice of bread and examines it from all sides. "Doesn't look too bad." She squeezes the crust between her thumb and index finger. "Hm," she says, before tearing off a piece and putting it in her mouth. She chews slowly, as though she's tasting the most delicate of products—to her, it is. And I can't believe it but, as I look at her, as I take in Jamie Sullivan in all her weary, unguarded glory—as I see who she is and who she has become—my wretched heart skips a beat.

CHAPTER 4

Jamie

"Thanks for coming." I let Mac into my room. She's dressed as though she's just come from the gym, although her skin is glowing and sweat-free. "Can I get you anything?"

"Just some water. It's going to be a long day and I want to go for a swim after this." She sounds casual, as though having this long overdue chat with me is just something to tick off her to-do list.

I grab two bottles of water from the minibar and lead us onto the balcony overlooking the ocean. The water is so blue it seems to dissolve into the sky.

"It's gorgeous here, isn't it?" Mac leans against the railing. "So colorful compared to New York."

"It sure is." Now that she's here, I no longer have eyes for the splendor outside. Even though it was a shock to see her on TV the first time, it was no surprise that Mac made it onto the daily news to cover sports. She has the kind of open, friendly face that no one can ever get enough of, that no living soul could ever mind seeing on a daily basis. "How are you, Mac?" I ask.

She turns to me and narrows her eyes. "I get why you didn't get much sleep last night. It's, um… a lot."

"Did you sleep well?"

"Only because I was exhausted with work and the time difference."

"You look well. You look…" Absolutely mesmerizing is what Gabrielle Mackenzie looks like. I can't even finish my sentence. How the hell am I going to give her the apology she so deserves? How am I going to clear the air between us? Is that even possible after all this time—and after what I did?

"What?" Mac asks.

"You look really good." I follow up my statement with a weird chuckle.

"Thanks. I'm kind of contractually obliged to."

Typical Mac to wave off a compliment about her looks like that.

"Look, Mac…" I try again. "I'm sorry for what happened and I'm sorry that I'm only saying this to you now." I wrote her plenty of emails I never sent and picked up the phone dozens of times to make a call that never went through. What I did was so shitty, I even lost the right to apologize—because a bunch of useless words could never make up for it.

She doesn't say anything, just briefly arches up her eyebrows and fixes her gaze on something behind me.

"Seeing you again," I say. "Part of me feels as though I shouldn't even be in this room with you. It's not how I usually feel, but… there's something about you. Something so intensely familiar and understandably distant at the same time. I don't really know how to act around you because of that."

The first sound to pierce the short silence that falls is a deep sigh from Mac.

"I don't want to sound like a cold-hearted bitch, but the truth is I don't care how you feel, Jamie. It took me a long time to figure out how to stop caring, but I did. In the end, I managed to stop loving you and what we had. If I seem distant, it's because of that. I had no choice."

Damn. I swallow hard.

"I'm here for Sandra, whom I care for a lot," Mac says. "For that reason, I can be perfectly civil to you, but that's all I can be. Seeing you again was always going to be perturbing, but I'm over that now. I'm not here to rehash the past. Maybe you had other ideas about what this conversation was going to be, but this is all it can be for me. Just so we're clear."

"Fair enough," I manage to mumble.

Before I can say anything else, Mac exits the balcony and heads inside the room.

"You're leaving already?" I blurt out.

"Why would I stay? What else is there to say?" She's not kidding about not caring one bit about me any longer. There's nothing but coldness in her voice and her friendly face is hidden behind a sheet of pure ice.

"I'm so sorry, Mac," I stammer. "I really need you to know that. I've always regretted what happened between us."

"Good to know," she says, before turning around and leaving the room. So much for having a conversation. Why did she even agree to a private chat? Probably because she couldn't say what she just said in front of anyone else. But again, I have no leg to stand on. When it comes to Mac, I have zero claims to make. And she has zero fucks to give, apparently.

I find the guys by the pool. They're drinking champagne already, and I'm tempted to join them, but it's a bit early —and it's Sandra's long-awaited wedding day.

Alan stares at me intently. "And?"

"And, what?" I sink into a lounge chair.

"How did your chat go?"

I shrug. "Badly." From under my lashes, I glare at the pool. Mac said she was going for a swim. She could pop up at the side of the pool, right in front of me, at any moment. I sit up a bit straighter. "Mission failed."

"What were you hoping to get out of it?" Charles asks. He wasn't around when Mac and I broke up—although breaking up is too gentle a term for what went down between us. When I callously destroyed our relationship of ten years, our wedding plans, and our future.

"Maybe some peace of mind. I don't know." I fill my cheeks with air and let it escape slowly. "Either way, Mac doesn't care, so nor should I. It's been too long. We're both different people now." I keep my gaze trained on the water. "Did you see her go into the pool?" I ask, just to be sure.

"She went for a swim in the ocean," Charles says.

Of course, she did. She's probably a mile out by now.

"What did she say?" Alan asks.

"It doesn't matter." I shrug. "We both agreed seeing each other again is quite distressing, but that's all it is." I'm not going to repeat what Mac said to me—ever, to anyone. "No residual feelings whatsoever."

"BS," Alan says. "Any fool can see that. Even this one."

"We can at least acknowledge that the whole experience was very different for Mac, and it still is now. I have to respect that." I inhale deeply. "Anyway, don't we have a wedding ceremony to get ready for?"

"That's hours away, darling." Alan doesn't pry further and takes another sip from his drink.

"In that case, I might rest my eyes for a bit." I suppress a yawn. I tossed and turned for hours last night, reliving the final conversation I had with Mac—the one in which I broke her heart into a million pieces. But there's no way I can fall asleep here with the hubbub coming from the pool and Alan's probing questions. I don't want to be alone in my room either, left alone with my thoughts and countless regrets.

"Hey, guys."

I recognize Sandra's voice so I open my eyes.

"Are you having fun?" she asks.

I'm in a five-star resort in Hawaii to celebrate my friend's wedding, yet I wish I was elbow-deep in some dough, kneading it to perfection, doing what I love the most. The lack of sleep is catching up with me and my non-conversation with Mac isn't helping matters.

"We sure are, darling," Alan says.

"Scoot over, please." Sandra taps my legs. I move so she can sit with us. "Did you go on a bender last night?" she asks when she sees my face.

"Just a little trouble sleeping."

She nods. It's the only explanation she needs. It's the only explanation anyone ever needs when it comes to Mac and me.

"I'll make sure to look my best this afternoon." I try not to imagine what Mac will look like—how dazzling and eye-catching she will surely be.

CHAPTER 5

Mac

I swim and I swim, until my arms burn so much I fear I might not make it back to shore. Being in the same room as Jamie, after all this time, was so disconcerting and threw me so off balance—especially when she started apologizing—that I had no choice but to hide behind a shield of bitter coldness.

We were never going to fall into each other's arms for a long-awaited reunion. She hurt me too much for me to ever be genuinely warm toward her again, but I surprised myself with the bite in my words, the sharp sting of them. So much for everything being water under the bridge.

I slowly make my way back, keeping my head above water so I know whether I'll have to avoid her on the beach. But I'll have to spend time with Jamie again in a few hours. We'll be sitting at the same table for hours tonight. Sandra did check with me before she arranged the seating plan and I said yes because I truly believed time had done its thing. Until I saw Jamie again.

I try to keep the memory of that soul-destroying emotion of loving and hating someone at the same time at

29

bay. Of not understanding what I must have done wrong to have her leave me like that. To have her dump me, three months before our commitment ceremony, as if I was nothing to her. Two decades later, I know for a fact it wasn't me. It was never me. It was Cherry—what kind of name is that, anyway? A cherry is a fruit you pick from a tree, not the name of someone you fall in love with when you're meant to marry the love of your life.

Jamie leaving me for Cherry had me in a state of devastation for months. The suddenness of it, the swiftness with which she said goodbye, stunned me into emotional ruin, just as I was going places—and making very detailed plans for our future as a couple and as a family. We'd have four kids if all went well. At least two. I would have been over the moon with just one baby to hold in my arms. But here I am, on the cusp of fifty, single and mother to no-one. That's what went through my head when Jamie started apologizing, when she said she had always regretted how things ended. I saw red because I might have come to terms with losing Jamie, but I never truly accepted not having children—and I somehow still hold her responsible for that.

I make my way out of the water.

"Looking good, Gabby," someone shouts. Someone always does.

I wave them off, not giving them a second look. I need to focus on myself, on getting my act together before the ceremony. I'll go through my routine of getting dressed and putting on makeup, as I do before I go on camera. It has a calming effect on me and surely sitting next to Jamie for the remainder of the day is less demanding than relaying the latest sports news to millions of viewers. *Yeah right.*

Without stopping to talk to anyone, I head to my room and start my ritual.

"I do," Sandra says. Tyrone, her brand-new husband, looks at her with so much love in his eyes, it touches something deep inside me. When was the last time someone looked at me like that? Or I at them? I can't even remember. I've never again come close to marrying. I've had flings and relationships, some of them even lasted a few years, but they always ended and although it most certainly wasn't always pleasant, no break-up has ever hurt me the way my split from Jamie did. Her dumping me so coldheartedly protected me from any similar future pain—maybe I should be grateful to her for that.

Next to me, Alan dabs a handkerchief against his eyes. There's wetness on my cheeks, too. Oh, damn it. This kind of glorious love on display is not missing its effect. I might have become a little bitter over the years when it comes to all things romance, but I'm not immune to this. To this union of Sandra and this other person she loves so deeply she wants to shout it from the rooftops. Thank goodness Jamie is sitting on the other side of Alan and Charles, because I really shouldn't be grateful to her for eternal protection against future hurt. She broke my heart so badly that, when I finally managed to put it back together again, it was no longer capable of a love like that —like I see in front of my very eyes right now. I can no longer imagine what it must feel like to love someone the way Sandra and Tyrone love each other. And boy, do I miss that feeling. Because I felt it every morning when I opened my eyes to Jamie lying next to me—always with a grin on her face, even at four o'clock. Every single morning I woke up and looked into her sparkly eyes, I knew she was the one for me, and I felt so disproportionally lucky to have found her, to be with her, and to have her love me back.

The tears keep on streaming. Everyone's standing up to applaud the happy couple. I follow suit. I'm not the only one crying—although, I suspect, none of us are crying for the exact same reasons. We're all projecting something onto this moment. I glance at Jamie, but I only see her back from where I'm standing. Her shiny shoulder-length hair that was so soft, I used to brush my cheek against it just for comfort, for the sheer pleasure of feeling it against my skin. Is it still so soft? I don't want to know.

Alan reaches out his hand to me and I gladly hold onto it. Beneath all his loud bravado, he's a big softie.

We collectively whoop as Sandra and Tyrone walk past us.

"Love you, San," Jamie shouts. "You too, Tyrone!"

I take a deep breath and gingerly dab at my eyes. I might need a few touch-ups before I'm ready for the group pictures, unless I hide in the back somewhere.

Jamie turns to us. Her cheeks are dry. We haven't exchanged many words since I stormed out of her room this morning, so it's still awkward between us, despite the boys' effort to diffuse things.

I send her a small smile.

"Are you okay?" she mouths. Even though I can't actually hear the words, I understand, because even though I believed—I hoped—I had forgotten, I remember so much. I remember everything. I remember how she used to silently ask if I was okay like that, her big, kind eyes instantly reassuring me, because Jamie always had my back—until she didn't.

I nod and look away because all of this shouldn't still be so painful. I was supposed to be over this. I *am* over this. Maybe I should have let that conversation earlier actually happen, let my emotions run riot for an hour or so, in order to deal with this wedding better. Because Jamie and I were getting married. It was all planned. The invitations were ready to go out so people could save the date. June 14th 2003 was going to be the most beautiful day of my life so far. Turns out, it was one of the most horrible, rivaling the day she confessed she was madly in love with Cherry and she couldn't possibly stay with me.

Why the hell is she wearing a tuxedo, anyway? It looks dashing on her, for sure, but she looks like she's dressed for her own wedding instead of attending a friend's.

"Come on." Alan's voice is surprisingly solemn. He curls an arm around my shoulders and Charles does the same to Jamie.

Alan holds me tight and for a woman who's never had a need for a man's arm around her, I'm thankful for the unexpected warmth of it. For the friendship he's giving me right now. For the strength I can draw from it. I'd never have guessed I'd need it so badly.

CHAPTER 6

Jamie

Even though Mac was so cold with me earlier, I can't for the life of me keep my eyes off her. She looks stunning in that red dress, with her hair slicked back like that. If Sandra were the kind of bride who cares about that sort of thing, she could accuse Mac of stealing her thunder, and she'd be right. Or maybe it's just me suffering from this strange affliction that has my gaze drawn back to her every few seconds.

Alan and Charles are masters at keeping a conversation going, even when they're seated between two exes and it's all a bit tricky.

Mac is being plenty nice and civil. The past couple of hours, the four of us have burst into spontaneous laughter a few times, making me wonder whether that episode in my room this morning actually happened. But this is what Mac does for a living. She dons her glad rags and puts up a front. That's what television is for.

"Which song do you think their first dance will be to?" Alan drums his fingertips against each other.

"I know what it's going to be," Mac says. "I introduced the song to Sandra and Tyrone."

"You?" I ask. When we first got together in college, I was the one making cool mix tapes for Mac.

Mac nods slowly.

"Don't keep us in suspense, darling." Alan all but pokes her in the arm.

"I'm sworn to secrecy, so don't even try to guess. The song's not been released yet. No one here apart from San and Tyrone—and me—will have heard it."

Alan's eyes go wide. "Is it a brand-new Isabel Adler song?"

"Nope," Mac says smugly. When did she become the person introducing her friends to new music? Did she develop a new interest after getting to know Isabel Adler via her ex, Leila?

I wish we could have a conversation long enough for me to catch up on her life of the past twenty years.

"But it's so gorgeous and kind of meta and just absolutely right for the moment," Mac says. "You'll see."

"You tease." Alan gives Mac a look of mock disapproval.

"Surely it won't be long now." Mac blows Alan a kiss. I'm a little jealous of how quickly the two of them seem to have gone back to how they were before everything fell apart. It's a million times easier when no romantic love— and heartbreak—was involved.

"I hope you brought your dancing shoes, darling," Alan says to her. "Because you and I will be on that floor as soon as we're allowed." Mac and Alan were always the first two on any dance floor. For all her questionable taste in music—at the time—Mac was always the sexiest dancer.

Come to think of it, I have no idea how I will react to seeing her on the dance floor, wearing that sensational dress. Despite knowing better, my heart skips a beat at the prospect. If only she didn't look so damn magnificent.

"Can't wait," Mac says. Then the moment arrives and the DJ calls the newlyweds to the dance floor. Sandra stands there beaming like the tropical sun while Tyrone thanks us all again for coming. The thought hits me out of nowhere. That this could have been Mac and me twenty years ago. Our commitment ceremony would have been much less glamorous, but that could still have been me, thanking our loved ones for celebrating our love with us. I'm taken aback by the powerful sense of deflation running through me. It's this wedding. It's all this love around us. All these happy people with their plus-ones. Even Alan has found himself an absolute stunner of a man to marry. Whereas I left the woman I considered to be the one for me for a fling that didn't even last a year. I threw away the greatest love I've ever known for what turned out to be not much more than a crush. A fleeting feeling followed by an avalanche of regret. Mac might not want to hear my apologies—and I can't blame her for that —but that won't stop me for being sorry for what I did. For what I squandered.

I glance at her from the corner of my eye. She has her gaze firmly fixed on Sandra and Tyrone, a gentle smile on her face. How can she still be the most beautiful woman I've ever seen? How is that even possible? She's so self-assured and poised. She didn't come close to breaking, not even a hint of a crack, when she was in my room today. Unless she fled at such speed to avoid it. The truth is that I don't know much about Mac any longer. All I know is that she's not the same woman I left twenty years ago. She can't be.

Sandra and Tyrone have assumed their positions on the dance floor. The first bars of Mac's mystery song play. Instantly, Alan clasps his hands to his chest—as though Isabel Adler herself has just descended from the heavens to serenade him personally. But it's not an Isabel Adler song. Is it? Since her comeback, Isabel Adler has a whole new style of singing, much more subtle and pared back— much more to my own personal taste, to be honest. It *is* an Isabel Adler song, but it's not her voice.

"Oh my god, kill me now," Alan says on a dramatic sigh, his voice close to breaking. "My favorite song in the whole wide world."

I recognize the words of Isabel Adler's biggest hit, "Somewhere I've Never Been", but the musical arrangement is completely different than the original as well as the phrasing of the lyrics, making it sound like a brand-new song.

"Who is that?" Charles asks.

"Shhh," Alan says, holding up a finger. "Later," he whispers.

Mac is swaying along to the gentle, slow beat of the music. She's as enthralled as Alan, but in a different way. I try to focus on Sandra and Tyrone, and on this new version of a musical evergreen, but my gaze returns to her again and again. She must have seen me look. What is she thinking? We used to joke that we were so merged, we could finish each other's thoughts as well as each other's sentences.

Mac's just enjoying the moment, though, and it's a beautiful moment. A wonderful celebration of that most elusive thing—for some of us, anyway—to hold on to:

love. Sandra and Tyrone look as though they're melting into each other. As though their bodies were made for each other, to move together to this song.

Tears stream down Alan's cheeks. It's beautiful, really, how he can be so touched by this and even more so that he doesn't give a damn about showing it. Charles rests his chin on his husband's shoulder and holds him from behind. Most couples around us are having a little private moment of whatever wonderful emotion is being coaxed from their lucky hearts. Mac and I are left to ponder things on our own. But as I live and breathe, I vow to ask her to dance with me later on, to a slow, romantic song like this one. It's all I want from this evening. One dance from the woman I used to love like no one else.

"Shoot me now," Alan says when the song ends. We all clap, which quickly morphs into cheers for Sandra and Tyrone.

"Am I allowed to speak now?" Charles kisses Alan on the cheek. "Aw, are you okay, babe?"

"It's just this beautiful full circle moment," Alan says. "Bianca Bankole covering Isabel Adler's greatest hit." He stretches his arm toward Mac. "Wow. I'm speechless, Mac. Best choice ever."

"I had very little to do with any of this." Mac takes Alan's hand in hers and gives it a squeeze. Did she swallow a lump in her throat? Now that I'm getting a good look at her face, it's obvious she's moved by this moment. Warmth blooms in my chest at the sight of her.

"Isabel Adler started recording again after her new partner, Leila, introduced her to the music of Bianca Bankole," Charles mansplains to me—even a kind man like him can't help himself. "It's all in her biography, which Leila wrote—and Alan has probably memorized by now."

"I read her biography, darling," I say.

"You did?" Mac asks, much in the same way I questioned her taste in music earlier. "You never liked Isabel Adler when we were together."

Alan shakes his head as though I've committed the biggest sin in the universe.

"Maybe not, but I sure was interested when she started sleeping with her female biographer."

Mac tilts her head as she looks me straight in the eye for the first time since this morning. Something shoots through me and I don't know if it's shame or guilt or something else entirely. This whole trip is so emotionally confusing, I'll need another vacation to recover from it.

Around us, more and more people are being coaxed onto the dance floor. It's only a matter of seconds before Alan and Mac make their move. I watch them go.

"Not keen on dancing?" Charles asks when we're alone. "I have terrible rhythm. I don't feel the music the way Alan does. It's just not in me. I need a bit more time before I can let go."

"I'll watch from the sidelines with you." I stare at the dance floor. Alan's twirling Mac around already. How the hell can she even stay upright in those heels, and why is she even wearing them? Didn't we used to rail against suffering from sore feet just because some man, who never had to wear an uncomfortable shoe in his life, one day decided women's calves look sexier when they're wearing heels? I do agree with whomever that man was, because Mac looks so fucking sexy, it's starting to tear me up inside —and not just because it makes me feel like a bad feminist.

"Has Mac said anything to you?" I ask Charles. "About me? About… us?"

Charles shakes his head. "We've only just met. If she had anything to say, she'd talk to Alan—although he would tell me if she had."

Mac has let go of Alan and is dancing on her own, arms in the air, hips shaking seductively.

"Are you okay, James?" Charles asks. "You look a bit… I don't know. As if you're decompressing already."

"Being here with her has thrown me for a massive loop. I didn't think it would still be so confrontational after all this time."

"The great loves of our life always are, no matter how much time passes," Charles muses, then throws an arm around me.

Loves, plural? If only, I think.

CHAPTER 7
Mac

Because I've had a few glasses of wine, I can at least pretend to dance as if no one's watching, although I can feel Jamie's eyes on me with every move I make. Throughout dinner, every time I glanced at her, she was watching me. My experience of sitting through hours of live sports broadcasting came in very handy when I had to pretend I didn't notice. And it is pleasing in some petty way, because part of me wants her to suffer a little when she looks at me, when she sees what she lost. That's why my hips have an extra sway right now. That's why, when I turn to our table, I let my gaze linger longer than I've done all day.

Oh, great. Teddy, Tyrone's father, is dancing his way toward me. The man's got moves and we are at a wedding, but he obviously also has a bit of a thing for me. Tyrone's mother is holding court at the main table, presiding over it like a queen. Maybe for that reason, Teddy just bops around me for a bit without striking up a conversation. This, I don't mind.

Although mostly pleasant, sitting at a table with Jamie

for the better part of three hours has been taxing. So I happily dance the awkwardness off me. Everyone on the floor is happy. The vibe is joyful. After a few songs, I may even say something to Jamie about this morning. About how big of a lie it was when I told her that I didn't care about her feelings.

"Come on, darling." Alan has waltzed up to me again and takes my hands. He twirls me around and, as I spin on my toes, I see Charles and Jamie make a tentative foray onto the dance floor. In our twenties, Jamie, Alan, and I spent endless nights in gay clubs, dancing until dawn. Sandra was often there as well. This reunion is a reminder of those happy times, a nostalgic trip down memory lane in more ways than one. After the break-up, Sandra and I still went dancing from time to time, but my friendship with Alan fizzled out, and I never wanted to see Jamie again. That we're all here tonight is mind-boggling.

Alan smoothly guides us closer to Charles and Jamie. Charles dances like a straight man, all awkward limbs and off the beat, which hardly makes him stand out at a wedding. Jamie's very different. She was always so much cooler than me, than anyone else I knew. She has this way of dancing that doesn't really look like dancing but still belongs on the dance floor. She's taken off her tux jacket and the stark white shirt she's wearing contrasts beautifully with the darkness of her hair and eyes. Maybe it's ancient muscle memory, or maybe it's something else, but I gravitate toward her. I can't help myself. We made so many ecstatic memories on dance floors together. Right now, because of the circumstances and the music and the joy around me, I can put the past twenty years aside, and just enjoy being here with her and Alan and Charles. It's a special moment that can possibly only exist in the magic

44

bubble of this dance floor, with the right kind of music in my ears, and the blissful vibes of Sandra and Tyrone's wedding around me. But the fact that this moment even exists, that, for a few minutes, maybe only for the duration of this song, I can forget what she did to me, the pain she put me through—the years of doubts about myself and the blow to my self-esteem—is nothing short of a miracle.

I smile at Jamie, and she smiles back. She has the kind of smile that lights up the darkest room. When I look into her eyes, I remember the countless reasons why I fell for her so hard. Why the prospect of marrying her and having a family together filled my heart with so much joy. Jamie and I always made such sense together, but it was more than that. When I was with her, I was free of doubts, free of second-guessing anything, because when I looked at her, I always knew that Jamie was my person. I trusted her completely. Even when we met Cherry and the three of us hit it off, like you sometimes do with someone you meet. Even when we started spending more time together, all I thought was what a great friendship the three of us had.

What a fool I was.

What a fool they made of me.

What a fool Jamie made of that great love of ours.

Then the reason I haven't been near her for twenty years hits me again like a ton of bricks. Why we haven't danced the night away together again. Why we never had a conversation ever again.

But I'm not leaving the dance floor to sulk in my chair. That's not why I came to Sandra's wedding. I came here despite knowing she'd be here. Despite knowing, although perhaps not fully wanting to recognize it, that it would do something to me. That I wouldn't be immune to seeing her again. That despite hating her, part of me will probably always love her a little as well. It's only for a couple of days. Then we'll go our separate ways. I might see Alan and Charles again although I can't be certain. So many promises are made at events like this that are never kept. Things are said simply because they are things you say. Alan's admiration of Isabel Adler is very real, though, and I sense he's not going to let his connection to her, via me, go anytime soon.

The music slows. The mood changes. The DJ puts on a slow song. Alan and Charles fall into each other's arms, as do most couples around us.

I look at Jamie.

She tilts her head. "Shall we?" She holds out her hands to me.

Oh. She's asking me to dance. I don't have time to think. I mean, I do. I can say no, but I don't. I owe her an apology, anyway, for my behavior this morning.

I nod and step closer. Finding a position for our hands is awkward. Mine end up on her sides while hers rest on my shoulders. With that wide gap between our hips, we must look like two shy teenagers dancing to their first slow song.

"Hey," she says. "You can still tear up the floor, then."

"Can you tell I haven't been out in ages?"

"Absolutely not." As we come back from a sway backward, she moves her hips a little closer to mine. "You look stunning," Jamie says.

I chuckle weirdly because I don't know how to react.

"I'm sorry about this morning." I'm acutely aware of her hands on my shoulders, her fingertips against my skin. "I was a bit harsh. I didn't mean to be."

"As I said." Jamie inches her head closer to my ear. "You never have to apologize to me." A pause. "Ever."

"It's just that, how I was this morning, that's not who I really am. It's not how I had intended to be with you." I had grand plans of being all gracious about the whole thing, but I guess those went out of the window the instant I saw her again. "It's not that I don't care, but I've had to find ways to move on. To forget you. None of those involved much kindness toward you."

"I shouldn't have tried to apologize. It was stupid. I'm sorry. Gosh. Now, I'm doing it again."

We might only have the presence of mind to mumble a few words to each other, but our feet move in seamless harmony, and our bodies inch closer together with every note of the song. As though our bodies remember something we can't allow our minds to.

"Let's just forget about apologies," I offer. "I'm curious... about you. About your life."

I know things didn't work out between her and Cherry. That it all fizzled out without much of a bang. I've never been able to decide whether that made me gleeful or sad. Is it better to get dumped for a great love—for a proper reason, for something inevitable—than for a flash in the pan? Two decades later, I still don't have the answer to that.

"You know me. I just love to bake."

"I've never bought anything Sully's Sourdough-related since then. I suppose I've been missing out."

Jamie tilts her upper body backward a little and looks at me with a smile on her face. "I couldn't watch the first Olympics you presented, but I did get over that. I had four years in between, so I had time to adapt."

How did she feel when she saw me on TV the first time? Nostalgic? Regretful?

We dance in silence for a few beats. I take the time to process some of the things that have been said. The song ends and another slow one starts. Jamie doesn't let go of me, and I don't let go of her.

"It's such a head fuck seeing you again, Mac," Jamie says after a while.

"I know." At least we're on the same page about that.

"Maybe we should have met up before coming here," she says.

"Yeah," is all I can reply.

"Would you have? If I had asked?"

"I don't know." Probably not.

"I've tried a few times over the years… to get back in touch with you."

"I made the very conscious decision to not respond to you after the first time. I couldn't. I didn't want to." I never wanted to see Jamie again, I was convinced of that.

Jamie's chin bops against my shoulder as she nods. I'm the one who moves in closer now. Her hand slides off my shoulder and finds mine. Our hips collide, then effortlessly find the rhythm of the music again. Then, somehow, we're dancing cheek to cheek.

"It might be a head fuck, but it's so good to see you," Jamie whispers. "It only hurts a little. You are still so gloriously you. Thank you for coming."

I'm not sure I can respond in kind. I'm glad I came, but I don't know how good it is for me to see Jamie again. It's a trip to dance so intimately with her. To feel her against me, to sense her body heat, to inhale her perfume —to know that her hair is still as soft as it ever was. Truth be told, it makes me want to hold on a little tighter—like my arms suddenly remember what they've lost.

Because I don't know what to say and neither does Jamie, we end the dance in silence. When the last note plays, it's hard to let go of her. But I do. Of course, I do—I have experience in doing so.

"Thank you." Jamie drops my hand. "I've got my eye on you for the next slow dance," she says, and turns away.

CHAPTER 8

Jamie

I've left the party and walked to the beach to cool off, to put some distance between myself and that dance floor where Mac is the center of attention. Good thing Sandra and Tyrone instated a strict no-social-media rule or Instagram would be filled with clips of Gabrielle Mackenzie letting her hair down.

The roar of the waves draws me closer to the shoreline. It's late, and most hotel guests have gone to sleep. To my left, a couple leans into each other while strolling on the beach. How lovely did it feel to hold Mac like that? When I told her it was good to see her again, I also meant that it was amazing to dance with her, to exchange a few words with her, to perhaps—or maybe that's just wishful thinking—witness the appearance of a tiny crack in her steel armor.

Giggles arise from behind a stack of lounge chairs. Three teenagers are smoking. When I look a little closer, I recognize them from the wedding party. They're Sandra's nieces and Tyrone's nephew, I think.

"Pssst." They beckon me.

It's really not my job to ask how old they are and whether they should be doing this. When I approach them, I smell weed.

"Want some?" one of the girls asks.

The brazenness of youth. They don't even consider that I could tell on them—not that I would.

"Weren't you canoodling with that smokeshow from the news earlier?" the nephew asks.

"Canoodling? I don't think so." I hold out my hand for the joint. Why not?

"Could have fooled me," one of the nieces says as she gives me the spliff. "It's strong stuff, just so you know."

I ignore her warning and inhale deeply. Like a middle-aged parent trying to be cool with her kids but failing miserably, I splutter out an embarrassing cough.

I shake my head. "I didn't see you here, but don't do anything stupid, okay?"

Light-headed, I walk back to where I came from. Those three young people could have been the kids Mac and I never had. We had our first IVF appointment booked for the week after our commitment ceremony.

"Instead of a honeymoon," she said. "But so much better."

She could have gone through with it on her own, but she didn't. Mac doesn't have kids and it's not because she can't have them. Or maybe she did get pregnant, and something went wrong after. There are so many possibilities. There are so many things I don't know. She's as much a stranger to me as those kids I just smoked with.

"There you are." Her red dress stands out against the darkness, that's how bright it is. "Are you okay?"

I don't tell her I just had a drag from a joint. *Wait.* Is she out here looking for me?

"I'm fine. How are you?"

Mac slants her head. "You look funny. Different."

"Must be the sea air."

"Hm." She can probably smell it on me—and she wasn't born yesterday. "Must be." She takes a step closer. "Do you need some water?"

I shake my head. "No, but thank you." I take advantage of the confidence that accompanies my light buzz. "Do you want to take a walk with me?" I ask.

"Hm. Yeah. Sure." She heels off her shoes and carries them in her hand.

"Great." I make sure to walk us in the opposite direction of the smoking kids. "Did you need a breather from dancing?"

"No. I'm in excellent shape," Mac says matter-of-factly, as though it should be obvious. It is. "But you'd been gone a while."

"You noticed?" I wouldn't ask so directly if I wasn't a little stoned, but here we are.

"First time in a room with you in twenty years, I'm going to notice, Jamie."

"Still. You could have sent Alan or Charles to find me." I'm pushing it, but I might as well. I may be high, but maybe I can also see this clearer now. We need a little push to get past these first few barriers of politeness and distance. There was a time when Mac and I were going to get married, for crying out loud. We should be able to have more than a superficial conversation.

"Can I ask you something?" Mac says, her voice shooting up a touch.

"Anything."

"Why did things not work out with you and Cherry?"

She's *really* asking me something. I guess what she

actually wants to know is whether it was worth leaving her for, to which the reply would be the most resounding *no*.

I try to laugh away my discomfort, but Mac has every right to ask me this question.

"It wasn't what I thought it was going to be."

"What did you think it was going to be?" Sounds like she's gone into journalist mode.

I huff out some air which leads into the most awkward chuckle ever. "I made a mistake." Only the biggest mistake of my life. "I excelled at being humanly flawed. I fell in love with another woman and instead of letting it go, of letting it fizzle into the nothingness it would eventually become, I left the love of my life. I left you." And I made everyone hate me, I don't say. My own father didn't speak to me for a month after I told him, that's how angry he was at first. He forgave me eventually, because he's my dad, but I will never forget that initial disappointment in his eyes.

"Are you still in touch with her?" If she's affected by what I just said, Mac's not showing it in her voice—or her line of questioning.

"God, no. It was... she was nothing. I mean, not nothing, obviously, but whatever I had with her was nothing compared to what I had with you. To what we had. You and me, Mac. It was everything and I blew it and I've had to live with that for the past twenty years." It must be the weed making me go down the self-pity route. With Mac of all people. "You had to live with it as well, obviously. I don't mean that my pain is comparable to yours because of what I did to you. It's not. I know that I hurt you so much and it's the biggest regret of my life. I know we're not supposed to do apologies anymore, but I want to apologize, because I've never been able to before and I'm so incredibly sorry, Mac."

"I think that…" Mac has slowed down. "The reason I don't want your apology is because I can't accept it. Because it doesn't change anything. Not then, and not now. What happened, happened. I can live with it now, but it took me a long time to not look for blame inside myself. For years after, I wondered if I had pushed you too hard or made you do or even want things you didn't really want. Because I couldn't for the life of me understand why you would leave me like that."

I swallow hard. My mouth is dry from the pot—or maybe from this suddenly very difficult conversation. The thing I hate about myself the most is exactly what she just articulated. That I hurt the person I loved most in the world. That I made her doubt herself.

"I was a fool," I say. It's still hard to actually say to Mac that I was in love with someone else.

"Was it really that simple?" She sounds as though, even though years have passed, she still can't quite believe that.

"There was nothing simple about it." I had the most excruciating choice to make. Leave the woman I'd had a wonderful relationship of ten years with, the woman I was going to marry and have kids with. Leave her for this exciting stranger who crossed our paths and choose a different life altogether. Cherry was seventeen years older than me and child-free. She was vibrant and eloquent and smart in all the ways that excited me. And she was fucking gorgeous. Maybe it was simple in the sense that I couldn't resist her. I tried so hard. I imagined Mac on our wedding day. I imagined her with our child in her arms. But then I would think of Cherry and my skin would break out in goose bumps and I'd have trouble breathing and my poor heart didn't stand a chance because it was under the influence of the greatest drug of all time: I was in love as well as in lust. I wasn't thinking clearly. The chemicals in my brain reduced me to a horny teenager with a one-track mind. It was horrible and amazing at the same time. Then, I slept with Cherry, and the choice was made. My fate was sealed. So was Mac's. "But it was not your fault, Mac. It wasn't anything you did or didn't do. It was all me."

"If years of therapy have taught me one thing, it's that it's never just down to one person when a relationship breaks down." Mac has come to a full stop. "Maybe Cherry coming along was a blessing in disguise. Maybe you and I weren't right for each other in the long run."

"My love life after you would very much suggest otherwise."

"I can't have been the one for you, Jamie. You left me."

"One does not exclude the other." The effects of the weed are starting to fade, but I can still say this to Mac. "It's never been the same with anyone else."

"Except with Cherry." Mac's voice is surprisingly demure—accepting even.

"No, definitely not with Cherry. In the beginning, sure." Although I was going through my own heartbreak as well, while falling deeper in love with Cherry. "But what you and I had was special."

"Maybe you're seeing our relationship through rose-tinted glasses. It was a long time ago." Mac drops her shoes into the sand. "Maybe it wasn't as good as we remember."

"I've made a lot of mistakes in my life and I surely

don't have all the answers, but there's one thing I know for absolute certain. You and I were exceptionally good together."

"We had our moments." Mac stares at her shoes in the sand. She hikes up her dress a fraction, then sinks down.

I drop down next to her, leaving a little distance between our legs, but not too much. "More than a few moments," I say. "We had ten beautiful years."

CHAPTER 9

Mac

"I liked Cherry too," I say. "I think you know that." It helps that I don't have to say this to Jamie's face. That I can stare into the blackness of the waves in front of me. "But I didn't sleep with her, let alone run off with her." Cherry Valenti was this whirlwind that raged through our lives. One moment, we had no idea who she was, the next, she was there all the time. She was the hurricane that destroyed everything and left our lives in ruins. It takes years to rebuild something from that kind of rubble.

"I did know you liked her," Jamie says.

We never said it out loud, but it was there in the undertones of our conversations. Meeting Cherry electrified our lives. Maybe our mistake was that we didn't talk about it, but we were planning a wedding, and I was preparing for my—hopefully—first pregnancy. That was not a conversation I wanted to have.

"You know what the very worst part of it all was?" My voice is so low, it's barely audible above the crash of the waves. "I was so angry with you, but... I also kind of understood. Not that you wanted to leave me and our life for her, but that you slept with her. If it had just been that, maybe we could have gotten past that. Together. These things happen. I never thought it would happen to us because... we were always good. We always had so much fun. Remember when we got our first sex toy?" An inadvertent smile breaks on my face. "We laughed so hard, it went unused for way too long."

"It's hard to forget, babe." Jamie clears her throat. "Sorry. I mean *Mac*."

"Since seeing you again, I've been bombarded with bad memories, but maybe I should try to remember the good times more. We had plenty of those and what's the point in raking up all this heartache, anyway?"

"Hm," is all Jamie replies. She clears her throat again.

"Are you okay?" I turn to look at her.

"Dry throat." She holds her hand in front of her mouth and coughs. "I might have had a drag from some kid's joint earlier."

"Are you kidding me?" This couldn't be more of a Jamie move if she tried. I shake my head, like we've gone back in time and I'm her spouse berating her for acting irresponsibly. God knows what she smoked. But I'm not doing that. I'm not her spouse and I'm also not that kind of person. If anything, I'd like to go and find those kids and have a few drags myself.

Jamie chuckles. "It was good stuff."

"Looks like it." I barely stop myself putting a hand on her knee. "I'll get you some water." I push myself up and pull my dress down. There's sand all over it.

"I'm fine. Let's go back inside." Jamie starts pushing herself up, but she wobbles and ends up with her ass back in the sand.

"Come on." I hold out my hand so I can pull her up. "You haven't aged as gracefully as I have."

"We'll see about that." Jamie puts her hand in mine and she's on her feet in no time.

I try to wipe the sand off the back of my dress, but there are spots I can't see.

"Can I?" Jamie asks. "Slap your bottom?" She grins her boyish grin at me. Next, she'll be sinking her teeth into her bottom lip and it will undo me a little—like it always did before.

"Yes. Thanks," I quickly say and turn my back to her —mostly so I don't have to see her face anymore.

Her touch is gentle as she brushes the sand off my behind. Whether her hand lingers is hard to say. What's easy to say is that it was cathartic to have this conversation with her. And to catch glimpses of this woman I used to love beyond measure.

"There you go, madam. Do let me know if I can be of any further service." Jamie's not done joking yet. I don't blame her. It's always easier to joke than to dredge up a painful memory.

"Shouldn't I return the favor?" I eye her backside.

"If I didn't know better, I'd think you're looking to get your hands on my ass."

"Been there, done that."

Jamie puts her hands on her sides. "Are you saying you don't want to cop a feel?"

"Are you saying that's what you just did when you were meant to be helping me?" Two can play at that game. That was always the thing with Jamie and me. We were so evenly matched in everything. We laughed at the same jokes. We wanted the same things. We both liked Cherry. Maybe the real drama, where things stopped being evenly distributed, was that Cherry liked Jamie more than me.

"As if you didn't know." She's doing it. There go her front teeth, delving into that luscious bottom lip of hers. Is she flirting with me now? Is she trying to compress the years we didn't speak to each other into that conversation we just had and move us past all the hurt, regret, and disappointment, just like that?

"My intentions were nothing but pure."

"In that case." A grin firmly plastered on her face, Jamie wipes at her behind. "Shall we go back in?"

I grab my shoes and follow her back to the party.

The celebration is still in full swing. Even though this is a small wedding, the dance floor is packed. Alan and Charles are shaking their booty with Sandra. I make a beeline for them, ready to strut my stuff again. I have some processing to do. I glance at Jamie who's standing by the bar, chatting to the bartender while rehydrating. It's hard to keep my eyes off her. Hold on. Is she flirting with the bartender right after flirting with me outside? She wouldn't. Or maybe she would. I don't know. Unlike what she told me on the beach. None of that was new information to me. Of course I know that she's sorry. And that it didn't work out with her and Cherry. And most of all, that what Jamie and I had was special. I just never gave her the chance to tell me any of it in person.

Without much further ado, Jamie walks away from the bar and joins us on the dance floor. If she was flirting—or being flirted with—it looks to be with zero consequence. I let it go because I'm here for a good time—and to replace some of the bad blood Jamie and I have between us with pleasant memories. Of these joyful moments dancing with our friends. Of the love we're celebrating. Even of seeing each other again and being able to talk to each other the way we just did.

This time around, because it's later, and because of our walk on the beach, Jamie and I dance differently with each other. Our bodies are more angled toward each other. There's more eye contact. There are many more relaxed smiles. Why wouldn't I smile when I see her like this? If I allowed myself such utter foolishness, I'd still be attracted to her. With her bangs that fall just below her eyebrows, drawing attention to her dark bedroom eyes. And that smile. Fuck me. I might as well still be attracted to her. But I'm not. I'm *really* not.

"Oh, Mac." Out of nowhere, Alan puts his arms around me. "I'm so happy to have you back in my life." He and Charles probably shared a bottle of champagne while I went out looking for Jamie. They seem very fond of the beverage.

"Me too, darling. Me too." As I say it, the music slows again.

"May I have this dance, Miss Mackenzie?" Alan asks, trying to keep a straight face.

"It would be my pleasure." Thank goodness the DJ hasn't put on an Isabel Adler song.

"What a fun wedding. It's sometimes hit-and-miss with these destination things where you don't know a lot of people, but this party's amazing," Alan says as we start dancing. It's very different dancing with him than it was with Jamie earlier. "Are you having fun?" he asks.

"I am. I'm glad I came."

"Did you consider not coming because of you-know-who?"

"Yes, but Sandra made it clear that was not an option if that was the only reason. She was right. It was time." From the corner of my eye, I see Charles dancing with Jamie.

"Where did you find that wonderful husband of yours?" I ask.

"Where do you think?" Alan laughs so hard, I can feel his body shake against mine.

"I truly have no idea."

"Grindr, darling." He arches up his eyebrows. "Of all places."

"Wow! Your hook-up turned into your husband. That's so great."

"He's a gentleman who's into loud guys. As soon as I realized that, I knew I had to hang onto him for dear life. We're that obnoxiously happy gay couple now. And we don't even sleep with other people. I never thought I'd see the day, but he's all I need." He smiles sheepishly, then narrows his eyes. "How are you doing in that department, darling?"

"What department would that be?"

"S-e-x," Alan mouths.

"I'm single," I say matter-of-factly. As if that answers his question. I know very well that it doesn't. I wouldn't want to deprive him of the satisfaction of grilling me a little.

"You're Gabrielle Mackenzie. You must be getting some."

He says it with such conviction, I can't help but chuckle—because he couldn't be more wrong.

"I'm really curious, Alan. How do you see my sex life? How does it work from your point of view?"

"I don't know. You turn up somewhere, looking absolutely gorgeous like you do tonight. You bat your lashes a few times and, boom, a few moments later, you're in bed with an equally gorgeous woman." He shakes his head. "I am but a simple man, Mac. I see that now."

"I don't think that works for anyone, of any gender, anywhere." Alan cracks me up and it's good to have a laugh.

The song ends and Alan bows to me as though I've done him the greatest honor of his life. From the other side of the dance floor, I see Teddy elbowing his way over to me.

"Jamie!" I shout.

As soon as she looks at me, I wave her over.

"I need you to dance with me."

Jamie tilts her head. "You do?"

"Argh!" Teddy has arrived by our side. "Am I too late?" He pretends to pout. "But who am I to come between two beautiful ladies?" He actually winks at me. "Enjoy your dance."

Jamie curls an arm around my waist and puts her hand in the small of my back. From the get-go, she pulls me much closer than before. Our hips touch and there's not an inch of space between our bellies. I rest my hand on her shoulder and she takes my free hand in hers, lifting it.

"Teddy did say we should enjoy ourselves." Jamie grins at me. "It's important to keep the father of the groom happy."

"Very important," I concur.

"In fact." Jamie folds her fingers around my hand and

starts leading the dance—any shyness she felt during our first dance together is long gone. "We should enjoy ourselves so much that he doesn't even think about interrupting us if there's another slow song after this."

"You always were a quick thinker, Jamie. Always coming up with all sorts of plans."

"If I remember correctly, you quite liked that about me." She presses her fingertips a little deeper into the flesh of my back. I can't say it's not having an effect on me.

"It's better than dancing with Alan while being subjected to questions about my sex life," I blurt out.

"Bless him." Jamie bursts into giggles and it's a surprising delight to feel her belly shake against mine. Instead of pulling me cheek-to-cheek, she rests her gaze on me. "But you can't blame the man for being curious."

"Are you fishing?" Who the hell am I kidding? I am still attracted to Jamie. She's the woman I've measured all other women against—and no one has ever come close.

Jamie nods. If she does that thing with her teeth again, I may succumb instantly—although there really isn't much to say.

"You go first." I'm not that easy.

Jamie huffs out some air. "My last relationship was a few years ago, actually."

"And?"

"And what?"

"You don't date?" I ask.

"I sometimes go on dates with myself. It's a thing now. Did you know?"

"Is that a euphemism for, um, you-know-what?"

Jamie snickers. "Are we having the same conversation?"

"I don't know. Are we not?"

"I told you I like to take myself out and you responded by asking if that's a euphemism for masturbation." Jamie does a full belly chuckle. "Damn. I forgot. This is what you're like. Good one, Mac." She shakes her head ever so slightly. "Fuck, you're a delight." She exhales deeply. Her face darkens, like she's suddenly standing in the shadow of something. She does pull me close now so I can no longer see her features. It changes the mood again.

Things have shifted from banter into something else, something deeper, something harder to deal with, especially at this time of night. Regret, probably. Good memories being crowded out by bad ones again because that's how it went—it's our story. We were good and then we weren't. And now we're dancing together and it's fun, but not the light, easy kind of fun because of all the baggage we carry. It's a bittersweet treat.

I push myself as close to her as I can because I may never get the chance to feel her body against mine like this again. I can do that now. I can allow myself at least this. Even though we're basically strangers now, it still feels a bit like coming home.

After a few moments, I realize we're barely still dancing. Our feet hardly move and our hips only sway lightly. We're holding each other in the middle of this dance floor, holding onto something we lost a long time ago. I don't even know if the song has changed. It's still slow and when I look up, I see other twosomes dancing together closely.

"I don't want to let go," Jamie whispers in my ear.

"I don't want you to," I reply. *What the hell?*

"We can't stay like this forever." Her breath is hot against my neck. "Once the music changes, this will not be a good look for us."

"Do you, um, want to talk some more? In my room?"

What am I doing by inviting her to my room? But it's a logical consequence of this evening—of this day and this trip. The alternative is going to bed and tossing and turning all night long, pondering all the questions I wanted to ask her but didn't get a chance to. Or wondering if it would have been fun to hang out with Jamie. Whether that was something I was capable of. Whether I've truly let go of the past and we can be a version of friends again.

"Very much so." Jamie's chin bumps against my shoulder. "Not to be funny about this, but it will look, um, a little weird if we both leave now after this dance."

"Poor Alan won't sleep a wink."

"Sandra's wedding night might be ruined."

"I can do stealthy. For the sake of our friends."

"Let's give it a few more songs. Then I'll say my goodbyes," Jamie suggests.

The fact that we're making this a secret rendezvous adds excitement to the whole thing. Unless Jamie thinks I invited her to my room for something other than continuing our conversation. That's not what I meant.

I think.

I'm sure.

CHAPTER 10
Jamie

I can't believe this is happening—or maybe there was only one way for this to go when Mac and I were finally in the same space again. Maybe it could only go how it always went between us. Because from the very first moment we met, more than thirty years ago, we've been drawn to each other. When I first clasped eyes on her in that dorm at NYU, I never wanted to look away again. And here we are, three decades later, with all that history between us, and I still only have eyes for her.

My intoxication is no longer an aftereffect of the weed I smoked earlier. It's all due to dancing with her, talking to her, just being near her. And I know it's all heightened by our circumstances. It all feels a little more intense than it might have if we'd bumped into each other back home— she'd probably have run a mile in the opposite direction.

"I'm exhausted." I hug Alan and Charles goodnight. I've already said my goodbyes to the bride and groom. "It's been a day and I didn't sleep very well last night."

Alan gives me a quizzical look. All that champagne

they drank might have caught up with his husband, however.

"Do you want me to tuck Charles in?" I ask.

"I don't need tucking in, James," Charles slurs. "Do you?"

"No, darling. Good night." I kiss him quickly on the cheek. Then there's only Mac to say a pro forma good night to. Unless she has changed her mind.

I put a hand on her bare shoulder. "Thank you for a wonderful evening," I say.

"And you." Mac smiles at me as though changing her mind about inviting me up is the last thing she wants to do. "Sleep tight," she says.

As I leave, I'm of half a mind to go to the beach and check if those kids with the weed are still there. It's a silly idea, but I'm nervous. Mac's invitation was ambiguous. I should have zero expectations, but it's impossible. On top of that, it really has been a long day. We've both had to process so many emotions. I should be locking myself in my room to decompress and catch up on the sleep I didn't get last night. But that's not what I want to do at all.

I let the door fall shut behind me. I don't know what to do with myself. Normally, I'd get undressed, but I still have a date. I still have to leave. I should have invited her to my room instead of agreeing to meet in hers. It would have been more practical. But I can't be doing any of the inviting or the instigating. I need to give Mac the space to make her own decisions. That's the only way it can be. How will I even know she's in her room? Will she—

There's a soft knock on the door.

"It's me," Mac says.

She's here? I quickly let her in. The first thing she does is rest her back against the door and kick her shoes off.

"That was quick." I can't help but smile.

"Alan and Charles called it a night after you left so I came up with them. It seemed easier to just come to your room." She looks around. The room is exactly as it was when she was here this morning, all too briefly. It seems like a lifetime ago.

I grab two bottles of water from the minibar and give her one. "Would you like to sit?"

There's a small couch by the window. We'd have to sit quite closely together.

"Hell, yes. My feet are killing me."

"Why do you even wear shoes like that?" I ask.

"Who the hell knows?" Mac sinks into the couch and drinks greedily from the water. "What a party. I'm so happy for them. What a dream wedding."

"Yeah." I position myself in the corner of the couch, but it's still so close to her our hips almost touch. "It was lovely."

"Does that include spending time with me?" Mac turns to me. Because of the cut of her dress, she has to sit with her legs pressed together—there's no hitching it up as she did earlier on the beach. Her knee touches mine.

"Very much so." I take a quick sip to swallow that sting out of the back of my throat. Sitting here with Mac is by no means difficult, but it's not easy either. It's something else. It's promising. Tentative. Progress, for sure.

"I—um," Mac starts to say something, then thinks better of it, apparently. "I'm not entirely sure why I came here. To your room."

"Maybe because…the night has been too beautiful to end. Maybe you want it to last just a little longer."

"That's definitely a part of it, but…" She sucks her lips between her teeth, like she's trying to bite her words.

She finds my gaze. I look into her bright blue eyes. "Oh, fuck it," Mac says, and puts her hand on my knee. Her fingertips dig in. "I don't know where you stand on this, but I would very much like to kiss you."

My jaw drops. Did I just hear that right or are my ears playing tricks on me—as in making my wildest dreams come true?

"I am very open to kissing," I say, mumbling the words, not sure Mac has understood them.

But she grasps my knee a little firmer. I angle my body so our lips have a direct path to each other. Although there's still a lot of distance to bridge.

Mac starts to lean in, but then pulls back.

"I need to say something first."

I nod. Say it quickly, I think, dreaming of her lips on mine. Hoping her touch will bring me some sort of absolution.

"I'm not drunk or under the influence. I'm doing this fully sober, but that doesn't mean this kiss is more than just a kiss. That's all it can be. Okay?" She's rambling. She's nervous. I get it.

"Okay." But of course it's not just a kiss. We also haven't even kissed yet. Mac is already protecting herself against something she might feel later—I do feel guilty about that. I put my hand on hers, run my thumb over her skin. I slide closer. "It's just a kiss," I whisper, before bringing the back of my finger to her chin and tilting her toward me. I look into her eyes, close the last of the distance between us, and touch my lips to hers.

I can't speak for Mac, but for me it's infinitely more than just a kiss. It's a moment of forgiveness. It's Mac opening herself up to me to such an extent I can barely believe it. I pull back. I open my eyes and look at her.

"Are you okay?" I whisper.

"Yeah." Her voice is as serious as her face.

I move in again, cupping her jaw with my palm, increasing the contact between us. My lips touch hers again, brief and light at first, but then Mac opens up to me even more. Her lips part. The tip of my tongue slides in, meeting hers. It's all so soft and gentle but inside me a tidal wave of emotions crashes through. Before tonight, this was never an option, not even in my wildest of wild dreams. I never dared to dream of kissing Mac again. All I wanted was for her to talk to me, for her to be able to look me in the eye and not just be reminded of the pain I caused her. This kiss is so much more than that. It's also totally different from any other kiss I've ever been a part of—because Mac's position is unique in my life.

Her hand is still on my knee, trapped beneath my own. She wriggles it free and brings it to the back of my head, pulling me closer. Her mouth opens wider. She's letting in more of me, and I welcome more of her. Our lips come together again and again and our tongues dance and as this glorious kiss progresses, pure joy erupts in my belly. But it's not just joy springing to life in my flesh. Mac's touch always ignited a deep arousal in me. It did so thirty years ago, twenty years ago and, apparently, it still does so now.

My breath becomes ragged. My free hand travels to her thigh, squeezing, feeling her. But I have to keep myself in check. I mustn't slide my hand up her dress. I want to so very badly, but it's not my call to make. So, instead, I push her backward onto the couch, while keeping my lips firmly planted on hers, and I straddle her. Her hands crawl up my back. Her tongue is hot in my mouth. This might still be just a kiss but it's a very different one than it was a mere minute ago.

I'm afraid to stop, to catch my breath, out of fear it will all be over as quickly as it began. That Mac will come to her senses, although she explicitly said she's fully sober. But just because she's not under the influence of booze or another substance doesn't mean she's not affected by the circumstances. I sure am. And I'm under the influence of her. The full human package that makes up Gabrielle Mackenzie. How incredible she looked when she walked into the party. How sexy she was when she danced. How direct she was in her questions. How unexpectedly flirty she was when we were wiping the sand off our clothes. How she held me when we slow-danced. How she said she didn't want to let go either.

But, fuck, I want this—her—so badly. I allow my lips to leave hers and kiss her lightly just next to the corner of her mouth. Then lower and lower. I trail a chain of kisses down her neck. In response, she throws her head back. She moans. Her fingertips dig into the flesh of my back.

I'm torn, but I have to ask. Verbal consent is absolutely required. We might have done this hundreds of times before, but that was twenty years ago.

"Mac," I whisper, as I look down at her.

She opens her eyes to me and sits a little straighter.

"Do you want to… stay?"

"I do," she says, like Sandra said to Tyrone earlier today, but in an entirely different context. She pulls me close and doesn't say anything else. Her mouth is too busy finding mine again.

CHAPTER 11
Mac

I'm not sure how unplanned this is on my part. I came up to Jamie's room. I looked her in the eye and told her I wanted to kiss her. I can kid myself a kiss is all I want, but it stopped being that the instant our lips touched. Because Jamie is Jamie—*my* Jamie. We were good at a lot of things together, but we excelled at this. Our chemistry was always very physical, and we always found each other again between the sheets—which made it hurt all the more when she slept with Cherry.

Kissing her doesn't take me back in time so much as it takes me out of time entirely. Back then, the second our lips met, the rest of the world seemed to disappear and, apparently, this hasn't changed. As though, even after all these years, part of her is still part of me. As though us being together, totally merged and codependent for ten full years, has weaved parts of her DNA into mine. Her touch is still electric. Her breath on my skin still feels as though a fire's being lit in my soul. Maybe some people are so important, leave such an impression, that the body can't forget them, no matter how hard the brain tries.

So, yes, I want to stay with her tonight. I want her to undress me, with her eyes first, then with her capable hands. I want Jamie to do to me what she used to do—because she always did it so damn well.

The past twenty years, I've dated amazingly interesting women. I've slept with people whom I found so sexy outside of the bedroom, I couldn't wait to get them into bed, only to find that this kind of spark, this thing I had with Jamie from the start, was so elusive, I had to conclude I could only ever experience it with her.

That's what killed me when she left me for Cherry, *after* she'd already slept with her. She must have felt that special spark that I believed was exclusively ours with Cherry, and that was the hardest thing to accept. The most difficult aspect to get over at first—before I realized that my dream of having a family with her got crushed as well when she left.

But despite all of that, despite Jamie leaving me and turning my life upside down, here I am. Her lips skate along my neck. Already, I can't get enough of her hands on me. Already, I want her with a passion I haven't encountered with anyone else—ever.

Jamie's growing in confidence with every kiss she plants on my skin. I can feel it. It radiates off her, and I want more, more, more. I want all of her. Just for tonight. These things happen at weddings, that's just a fact of life. Especially at destination weddings in romantic locations like Hawaii. I can accept that—and I can use it as the perfect excuse tomorrow.

Jamie looks down at me again. Her eyes twinkle and she traps her bottom lip between her teeth. It makes her look irresistibly mischievous. With her gaze pinned on me, she starts to unbutton her shirt. My mouth goes dry at the prospect. My eyes are glued to her hands, her nimble fingers. She opens the sides of her blouse and reveals her chest to me.

I reach out my hands and slide them from her belly to her back. Her skin is warm and inviting. I can't wait to explore every last inch of it. To find out what has changed about her and what is still the same. Because I once knew this body like the back of my hand. I charted every freckle, every bump on her skin, that tiny, nearly invisible birthmark in the crook of her arm. I open her bra, slide it off her.

Her breasts don't look the same—how can they?—but they still take my breath away. Her tiny nipples are rock hard. Instinctively, I reach for them. Jamie leans over and I skate my tongue along her nipple while I cup her other breast in my hand. A riot starts between my legs. My clit throbs. The fierceness with which I want her surprises me —maybe even scares me. Perhaps because this shouldn't feel as good as it does. It should be more awkward, less fluid and effortless. Because so much time has passed. But time stops now that I have Jamie's nipple in my mouth, and she moans deep in her throat—like she always did— and it sets something off in me.

My body remembers how it loved hers. How it could never get enough of her. How it tried to keep her in bed when Jamie's alarm clock went off too early. How it held onto her—long after she'd left. How our bodies fitted together so seamlessly, as if they were meant for each other. No wonder my body brought me here. My feet carried me to her room. My lips formed the words that declared my intention. It's a far cry from how I felt this morning, when I was in this same room, and when I was met with an avalanche of pain. It's miraculous what a few hours and a bit of conversation can do. Seeing Jamie as more than her betrayal changed the circumstances so much that it led to this.

Jamie twists her torso away from me, but my mouth doesn't have to go without her long. Her lips are back on mine and the earlier tentative gentleness has made way for Jamie's tell-tale determination. Her hands wriggle between my back and the couch. She's probably trying to find the zipper of my dress. My bright red eye-catching dress that I picked for a reason. Because I wanted Jamie to look at me. It was expensive but totally worth it.

"Let's move to the bed." Jamie's voice is sultry and low. She climbs off me and holds out her hand. It's only a few steps to the foot of the bed.

I point her in the right direction to the zipper. Jamie wastes no time sliding it down. Her hands are warm on my shoulders as she guides the fabric off me until it's nothing but a messy red puddle on the floor. I swallow hard because I'm standing in front of Jamie in just my underwear.

"You're so beautiful," Jamie mutters under her breath, but I can still hear it clearly. She undoes the button on her pants and steps out of the tuxedo bottoms she has worn so well all night.

The sight of her feels like slamming into a wall of heat. Her soft dark hair falls to her shoulders. Her pale skin contrasts with the black fabric of her underwear, which is more practical than sexy—it always was. Why would she wear sexy underwear, tonight of all nights, anyway?

While we used to always keep things light and even jokey when things got hot under the collar, there doesn't seem to be much room for that tonight. Maybe because there's something utterly fragile about the whole situation. Although, I don't feel as though I'd bolt out of the door if one wrong word was uttered. There are no more wrong words, and I've thought the worst of Jamie for the better part of two decades already. I'm ready to let go of all of that, even if just for one night, to be free of that burden, that sadness that's burrowed its way deep inside of me. I want to replace the bitterness I've associated with her with a new joyful memory. Then move on again, free and lighter.

Jamie makes a move for me. She won't be able to stand that I'm still wearing a bra while she isn't. That I've had my hands and lips all over her breasts while she hasn't touched mine. Who am I to keep her waiting? My bra is disposed of in seconds.

"You're so fucking sexy," she says, articulating very clearly now. And I believe her. Not that I have trouble believing that I'm sexy in general, but I believe I'm sexy to her. That she once again wants me with every fiber of her being.

When you love someone with all your heart, when you want them with all that you are, and the other person doesn't want you with the same passion, that's the most humiliating, demoralizing, devastating feeling in the world. That sort of thing will break your spirit for a good long while. Then you get over it, because life goes on and time does its thing, but something always lingers. Nothing's ever quite the same again. You're always slightly off balance. Not a lot, not so much that it messes up your life forever, but just enough to make you remember that you once had something special and you're not quite sure you'll ever feel like that again.

Come tomorrow, I'll probably revert to that feeling

again. But that's why we have tonight. That's why my soul feels momentarily restored when Jamie says I'm sexy. But that's also why she can only say this now, in this room, when it's dark outside, after the day and evening we've had. At this wedding, where a friend brought us together. This is the only moment in which this balance can exist. I know that. And I'll take it.

Next thing I know, she's pinching my nipple between her fingers, which is always a direct line to my clit. I haven't been this turned on, this ready for everything, in years, maybe decades. Maybe since the last time we slept together, when I had no idea she was slipping away from me, that I was losing her to someone else.

Jamie smiles at me now. She paints on that devilish grin I remember so well. The one that always undid me. The one that said loud and clear, *I'm going to make you come so hard, you won't remember what day of the week it is.* Jamie was always very good at that. She had me weak at the knees from the first day we met. I tried to play hard to get, but I've never been as useless at anything as I was at that.

She pushes me down onto the bed. My panties slide off me a fraction and I get rid of them entirely.

Jamie looks at me. Her devilish grin has morphed into an amused smile. She follows suit, and then I'm fully naked in bed with the ex that hurt me the most. I'd never thought I'd see the day, yet it somehow makes perfect sense.

"Hi." Jamie's voice is all warm, liquid lust. She kisses me again, and suddenly her hands are everywhere. Jamie's all over me and every muscle in my body surrenders to her. My body has only waited twenty years for this. When her lips close around my nipple, I almost come there and then. Just from the delicious shock of it all, and the relentless desire that's been building inside me. From seeing her naked. From feeling her body against mine. From being estranged from her for all these years to this.

The contrast is stark and stunning and overwhelming. Everything about Jamie is overwhelming, almost too much, but not quite. And that's because Jamie Sullivan is —was—just right for me. That's why it never got old between us. We managed to keep this delightful tension between us throughout the years. I'm not saying it's still there—the only thing that's still there are memories, half of them probably not even accurate. But nostalgia is a powerful force and her body against mine is the most poignant of all because it always was the essence of us. We were always touching, always walked down the street holding hands or with an arm slung over the other. It didn't occur to us to not always be in physical contact, to not be intertwined.

Her lips travel to my mouth again because she can't seem to get enough of kissing me. The feeling is entirely mutual. While we kiss, her hand drifts down to land between my legs. Her fingers trail through my wetness and I so want to hold on. I desperately want to hold out for that no doubt magical moment when her tongue touches against my clit but, for the life of me, I can't. I can't control myself. My body does what it wants to do most. Submit to Jamie's touch. It only takes a few ridiculously light strokes against my clit for my entire being to yield to her.

With Jamie's lips on mine, our tongues slow-dancing— like we did on the dance floor earlier—I come exactly as hard as she implied I would.

CHAPTER 12

Jamie

Mac is so goddamn beautiful, I could cry. But I keep my tears at bay. To have her come like that means a lot to me, but it must mean something to her as well, and I want her to have this moment without me pushing my emotions onto her.

"Jesus fucking Christ." Yep. She still swears like a sailor—but only ever in bed. "Do you have magic fucking voodoo fingers or something?" She pulls me to her.

"Only baker's hands." I smile down at her. Making her come like that surely earned me the right to kiss her again, so I do. Mac pulls me even closer—as close as I can possibly get. My skin melds into hers, my flesh is on fire. Mac turns me on excessively because as much as it wasn't just a kiss, this isn't just sex. I can't know what it is to her—maybe she will tell me later, maybe she won't—but to me it's part redemption, part certainty that there are so many good reasons why Mac and I made such sense together.

My clit is a red-hot fireball between my legs, but all I really want to do is make Mac come again. I want to taste her, feel so much more of her. But maybe she needs a minute or two. I'm sure she'll let me know.

While I kiss her, my hands keep caressing her body. It's familiar but it's also not. Twenty years change a person inside and out. I sure have changed—at the very least, I've seen the error of my ways.

Mac pushes up her knee. I press myself against it. I might be heading for an early release just like she did. If I keep rubbing against her like this, while her tongue dances in my mouth and her fingertips dig into my flesh, I might very well come within the next minute. I wouldn't call it a premature climax, because it's been building all weekend. From that very first hug, which was stiff and awkward, but still. It was the beginning of this.

Mac retracts her knee, leaving me hanging in more ways than one. I open my eyes. She has a smug smile painted on her face when I look down at her.

"Are you still orgasmic popcorn?" she asks.

I chuckle. "Why don't you find out?"

"Gladly." She looks deep into my eyes and I'm caught off guard by a memory of us in stitches in our bed—the one with the really shitty mattress in that fourth-floor walk-up in Williamsburg. Of Mac laughing so hard, she fell out of bed and sprained her wrist. Even though painful at first, in the aftermath it was mostly funny because we knew how she'd hurt herself and the bandage around her wrist was a constant reminder.

"Are you okay?" Mac's voice is so tender, so caring, it would floor me if I wasn't lying down.

"Yeah. This is kind of a lot. You're not just anyone." For ten years, Mac was the most important person in my life. The one whom everything revolved around.

"I know. It's… unexpected." She brings the back of

her hand to my cheek and caresses it softly. "Are you still okay with this?"

Am *I* still okay? I might be emotional and a little over-whelmed, but I'm more than okay with being in bed with Mac. I can't claim it was the first thing on my mind when I saw her again, because to even entertain the prospect felt wrong. Yet here we are—and it feels so incredibly right.

I nod. "Are you?"

"I just came quicker than a horny teenager, so yeah. I'm pretty good."

"Not bad for a woman who's about to turn fifty." I've never forgotten Mac's birthday. It's always been a weird day for me.

"Let's see what it's like for a woman who has already celebrated the big Five Oh." With her strong body, Mac flips me off her and has me pinned beneath her in a matter of moments. "What did you do for your fiftieth?"

"Can I tell you later?" I smile up at her. My clit is still pulsing like mad and Mac flipping me over like that has only made it worse. "I'm a little preoccupied right now."

"All right." She narrows her eyes to slits, then closes them completely before she leans in again. Mac kisses me and my body surrenders to her touch completely.

Her arms are strong and solid when I run my fingers along them. Mac was a college athlete, and her sexy arms were one of the first things I noticed. Thirty years later, I still get the same kick out of them. Or maybe that's just because they belong to her, to Gabrielle Mackenzie—the love of my life. The one I squandered.

Even though every fiber of my being is screaming for release, I could stay in this position, cradled in her soft embrace, for a good long while to come. With Mac draped over me, her lips on mine, our hands all over each other.

But then she tears her lips away from mine. She traces a wet path down, stopping at my breasts. When I catch a glimpse of her gaze, it's more serious than sparkling. More filled with intention than wittiness. She licks along my nipple and a fresh fire is stoked in my core, adding to the one I already had going. It's not just lust speeding through my flesh. It's pure happiness because it's Mac's tongue against my skin, it's her knee pushing my legs apart.

If I have one superpower it's to enjoy a moment when it presents itself. To block out most of reality and just go for it. In this instance, because of our muddled history, the utter bliss of the moment, of this short night we have together, threatens to escape me a few times, but I can pull it together. All I need do is look down at what Mac's doing. Mac and I are having sex, which feels more like a miracle than anything else. Her lips meander down, pressing on my skin, surely leaving their imprint on me forever. She settles between my legs and I can't just lie back, close my eyes, and enjoy what's about to transpire. I have to look. I need to see her.

She gazes up at me briefly with those eyes I used to know so well. Those eyes I only ever needed a brief look from to know what was up. They are a mystery to me now. Since I left, Mac has lived another life without me. I have no idea what's going on inside her head, although I can easily tell she's enjoying this just as much as I am. She wouldn't have come so quickly if she wasn't, if she wasn't so turned on by my 'magic voodoo fingers'. For all that we've lost, we still have so much between us. And my silly brain can't help but go there—can't help but dream of what lies beyond this moment and this night. It's stronger than me, but then, luckily, Mac's kisses on my lower belly grow more intense, and my brain stops working.

I become all ragged breath and tensed-up muscles. I am made of nothing but the most divine anticipation. This is perhaps the best moment of all, that instant just before Mac makes me explode. Because it's all there in this moment. This weekend, all the years we had and all the ones we didn't. Our difficult and easy conversations. The coming together on the dance floor of all places. Our walk on the beach in the dark. How magnificent Mac still is after all these years. How easily I could fall for her again, just because she's there and that's really all it took the first time as well. I saw her and something inside me shifted, something deep inside me knew that girl was special. That a move had to be made. Many moves were made, not all good and not all bad, and we didn't make it in the end, but how I'd love a shot at another chance. Oh, how I want to make things right with Mac. How I crave her absolution. How I want her to tell me, and mean it from the bottom of her heart, that I have been forgiven for making the biggest mistake of my life. But just like I knew deep down when I met her that she would be very special to me, I now know that this will never happen. She might be able to forgive me—she may already have—but the damage I caused can never be undone. Life can't be rewound. Regrets can be lived with, but the course of a life can't be altered after the facts.

So, it's not just pure bliss blooming in my heart after all. There's an edge of remorse, of bitter pain, clinging to it. Although, somehow, the life we've lived, and the people we've become to each other because of it, casts a particular kind of light on this moment. It takes a special kind of intimacy to so easily come together again after all these years. We'll never again be the Mac and Jamie we once were, but we are this version of us now.

Mac sure does take her sweet time, but her lips are approaching. I groan with anticipation. How long has it been since I felt her tongue there? How long have I wanted to feel it there again? I don't know the answers to any of these questions. And—oh.

It's as though someone unplugs whatever was holding me together up until this point. As soon as Mac touches my clit, my muscles go slack, my bones melt into my flesh. I sink into the mattress while my body releases years and years of pent-up emotion. All the shame. All the guilt. All the regret and hurt. It all catches up with me as her tongue skates along my clit. What follows next is more an exorcism than an orgasm. An expulsion of the pain I caused her but also myself. It's the bottomless regret I've lived with for all this time transforming into something more bearable. It's all the feelings I've had to suppress in order to get on with my life clawing their way to the surface, not to wound me, but to exit my system once and for all.

Then I do cry because tears are a big part of this too. All the tears I didn't allow myself to cry because I was the one who fucked up. I was the one who made the choice, so I had to grin and bear it.

"Hey, sweetheart." Mac calling me sweetheart only makes me cry harder. "Oh, god. Oh, come here." She crawls up to me and pushes her warm, comforting body against mine. She holds me in her arms and whispers sweet nothings in my ear just to soothe me. She's so kind, just like she always was. I used to jokingly ask her how someone as hot as her could also be so kind—as though one would exclude the other. It was a joke then, but it's not very funny now. Because kind is the very last thing Mac should ever be to me again.

CHAPTER 13

Mac

Instead of a pounding hangover, which I'd expect after a wild wedding party, I wake up with a throbbing between my legs. My body aches in places I didn't even know I had muscles—me, a former athlete and current sports journalist. It's my job to know about the human body and its limits. My own body was stretched far beyond its limits last night. After that first quick climax, I might as well have been the orgasmic popcorn Jamie used to be. She was all over me for the rest of the night, as though she wanted—needed—to make up for twenty years in one night.

I turn onto my side. Light peeks from underneath the curtains, but Jamie's still sleeping. To witness her fall apart like that was the most remarkable thing to have happened since I've arrived here. She regrouped quickly enough, but still. I was with her for ten years and I've never seen her do anything like that. She's not the kind to break down like that.

I can't resist running my fingers through her hair. I'm glad she's not awake yet because it gives me a moment to ponder what this is between us. I remember what I said last night. *It's just a kiss.* That was my first lie. To think that what happened in this bed was just sex would be another. It's not possible for us to just have sex. If only it hadn't been so damn good. If only Jamie couldn't still play my body like it's all she's ever done in her life. If only she wasn't so damn sexy and desirable, because it clashes greatly with all the other things I feel for her. But I can't claim to hate her any longer. That wasn't hate sex. Nor was it makeup sex. It's way too late for that. I don't really know what it was beyond, maybe, reunion sex. Nostalgia mixed with all the other emotions a wedding can unearth in a person. I settle on that. Because that's all it, ultimately, can be.

"Morning." Jamie's face breaks into the biggest smile. "Wow," she whispers.

"Yeah."

"You're still here." She catches my hand between hers and holds on to it for dear life, as though I might still make a run for it now.

"Do you want me to go?" I ask, knowing full well it's the last thing she would want.

Jamie shakes her head. "I want you to stay here all day long."

"We're in Maui. We have to see the sights." It's a hell of a long flight from New York to Hawaii. The inside of a hotel room isn't all I want to have seen before I go home, although a hotel room with Jamie Sullivan in it could probably sway me. But no. Hard no, actually.

"How long are you staying?" Jamie asks.

"One more night. You?"

"A week." She pulls her lips into a pout. "You came all this way for three nights?"

"I couldn't get more time off."

"Couldn't or wouldn't?" Jamie asks. How does she know? She used to be the bread-obsessed workaholic, not me.

"Doesn't matter. People are counting on me being back at the studio on Wednesday."

"Are you saying you're a big deal at ATC?" Jamie threads her fingers through mine.

"I'm a very big deal," I half-joke. It's ironic because the only reason I became so successful is because I haven't had much of a life outside of work. When you don't have a spouse and children, you can work as much as you like. You can become the one person the producers know they can always rely on, because no one else is relying on you.

"I wish you were staying longer," Jamie says.

"Why?" It's not that I want to kill the mood, but something needs to be said.

"To spend more time together. We have so much to catch up on."

"Jamie, um… last night was fun, but I don't want you to get the wrong idea. This is not a thing."

"No. Of course not. I wasn't implying that it was. I just… would have loved to spend some more time with you. Is that so weird?" Jamie keeps her cool, which is rather attractive. "You're such a wonderful person, Mac. And your tongue… Hm." She arches up her eyebrows and nods slowly. "Top notch. No wonder I want some more of that."

I admire her for keeping things light. I seem to have more difficulty doing that. "Seriously, though, Jamie."

"If you don't want to see me today, that's fine. If you want to pretend last night never happened, that's also fine. Anything's fine with me, Mac. I'm just glad that…" Her voice trails off. Oh, there she goes again. She sucks part of her bottom lip between her teeth. It makes her look vulnerable and irresistible at the same time. "I don't know. The sex was unbelievable, like mind-blowingly so. It was for me. And I know this isn't a thing, whatever 'a thing' may be, but it sure as hell wasn't nothing to me."

"It wasn't nothing for me either." I can't lie to Jamie about that, although maybe I should. But that would be impossible. "It was unbelievable, actually, but... well, I guess it could have gone either way. It could have been awkward and unfulfilling, but it went the other way. Maybe it was something we needed. Maybe it was the only way we could put some things behind us. I really don't know." I'm babbling now. I have no idea how to summarize last night, or this weekend. It doesn't matter any longer whether ending up in bed with Jamie was a great or a horrible idea, because it already happened. And it was spectacular. But that doesn't mean I want to—or should—do it again.

Jamie smiles softly at me. She looks angelic. She's still as gorgeous as ever. "How about we order some breakfast and see where the day takes us? What are those sights you're talking about that we must see?" Under the sheets, her hand snakes toward my belly. Her fingers slide across my skin until my breast rests in her palm. She was always so deliciously audacious—no wonder Cherry picked Jamie over me. Damn. That's the first time since I opened my eyes that Cherry has entered my thoughts. It's not ideal, but it is a reminder of why this is the way it is. "Did I tell you that your breasts are the most glorious sight I've seen thus far on this island?" Jamie moves in and I know I should stop this right here and now, but when she gets physical, when her magic hands are on my body, it's impossible.

I can't help but chuckle either, because Jamie's so silly and sexy at the same time. Some things never change.

After another climax, Jamie and I have breakfast on the balcony, overlooking the shimmering blue of the Pacific Ocean.

"Alan will go nuts if neither one of us shows up for breakfast," Jamie says.

"Or maybe he has his hands full nursing Charles's hangover." I take a sip of coffee.

"We probably shouldn't tell them about, um, this. Alan won't be able to process it and he'll make a big deal out of it. You know what he's like."

"My thoughts exactly," I agree.

"I might tell him when we get back, though. Is that all right?" Jamie asks.

"I guess."

"He's pretty keen to rekindle your old friendship."

"Mainly so he can meet Isabel Adler, but yeah, I would like that, actually. Don't worry, I can deal with Alan."

"Isabel Adler's not the only reason Alan would like to see more of you, Mac. You do know that, don't you?"

"Yeah. Sure."

Jamie rips pieces off her croissant and examines them closely before popping them into her mouth. We eat in silence for a few minutes. I can feel the lack of sleep catching up with me. "I think I may need a few more hours of sleep before seeing any sights." I stifle a yawn. "You were relentless with my almost-fifty-year-old body."

Something crosses over Jamie's face. It can't be the shadow of a cloud because the sky behind her is a pristine blue. "Do you think we could meet up when we're back in New York? Maybe go for coffee?"

Yes. No. I don't know. How can something be such a good and a bad idea at the same time?

"You don't have to answer now, but maybe I can call you sometime when we're back home?" Jamie arches up her eyebrows. She's only wearing a robe and it's sliding off one shoulder—making me want to say yes very much. "Do you still have the same number?"

"You know I don't." Because I never wanted to hear from her again, I changed my number not long after she left.

"My number hasn't changed," Jamie says. "How about you call me if and when you want to?"

"You think I still have your number?" It comes out a little harsher than I want it to.

"You don't?"

I shake my head. After the first shock had subsided, I purged my life of all things Jamie. I got rid of all the stuff she left behind, including all the things we'd bought together, and I started fresh. I had to. And I could no longer stand the thought of having her number in my phone, as though it could hold only a limited amount of numbers and hers being part of that select group was taking up precious space—as though her name being in my phone contaminated it somehow. Why would I ever call her again, anyway?

"Can I give it to you?" Jamie asks.

"No need." I chuckle. "Remember when we got our

first mobile phones?" That's how long ago Jamie and I met.

"Yeah. Crazy, right?"

"Let's see if my memory is as good as I believe it to be." I close my eyes so I can focus, then I rattle off her number.

"Color me impressed." Jamie's eyes have gone wide. "You remember my phone number!"

"I memorized it back then and I guess my memory is fully intact." I want to say that I don't remember the number specifically because it's hers, but what's the point of clarifying that? And I do actually remember. The things our brains choose to hold on to.

"In that case, I'll look forward to your call."

"We'll see." It's all I can say because I don't know if I want to have coffee with Jamie. Maybe it would be different if I hadn't slept with her—and if it hadn't been so damn satisfying.

CHAPTER 14

Jamie

I nstead of seeing the sights she claimed she so desperately wanted to see, Mac stayed in her room most of the morning, and was lounging by the pool for the better part of the afternoon. It's coming up to dinner time and Alan and Charles, who did get an excellent night's sleep, have their eye on a beach-side bistro as the venue for our saying-goodbye-to-Mac dinner.

I'd love to have Mac to myself tonight, and a good long while after, but I have no idea what she wants—and the ball's firmly in her court. I made my intentions clear when I said I wanted to spend time with her and I'd like to meet up in New York. That's all I can do.

I'm strolling on the beach when my phone beeps. It's a message from a number that's not stored in my phone.

> Those gays are relentless about having dinner. 😅

It must be from Mac. My heart skips a beat. My phone beeps again. A new message rolls in.

> I can't tell them my body can't cope with a near-sleepless night any longer.
> Imagine the interrogation I'd be subjected to.

I text back:

> Sorry-not-sorry for keeping you up all night. 😊

Last night was like a dream. If I didn't have these messages from Mac on my phone referring to it, and confirming it really happened, I'd be questioning my sanity. I actually slept with Mac. Alan might not be able to process this information, but he's not alone.

When we woke, Mac didn't hurry out of my room, saying it was all a big mistake. We even had breakfast together on the balcony. It was all so much more than I could ever have hoped for. Of course, I want more, because sleeping with her was sublime—both because we are former lovers and because there was an exciting novelty to it nonetheless. But I may very well want that now, in this dreamy location, surrounded by romantic wedding vibes, away from my normal life, but who knows how I will feel when my feet touch down on New York soil again?

Another message announces itself.

> I'll see you and the gays for dinner in an hour then.

If I asked Alan, he'd happily give me the chance to dine with Mac alone, but we promised not to tell him and

Charles. Come to think of it, I wonder why. We're all adults.

"Hey, lady!" One of the potheads from last night shouts at me. With two fingers, he makes a smoking gesture.

I wave him off. That was last night. That was *before*.

I clearly remember Mac's words of this morning. "This isn't a thing." Maybe we should start by defining 'thing'. Or maybe it can only be ambiguous. Because there's so much history between us. So much pain, but also so much love. If only it hadn't been so much fun, so thoroughly and utterly fantastic—despite me breaking down in her arms. But maybe that was exactly what I needed so I can finally wipe that slate clean. And even though I know very well the ball is in Mac's court, maybe I can at least admit to myself that I would love to see her again in New York. That I'd love to do much more than go for coffee. That I'd like to take her on a date. Spend another night with her. That I'd like to make it very clear to her that seeing her only confirmed what I've known all along. That leaving her was a huge mistake and that I would give anything for another chance. To find out if we're still so good together.

Part of me also knows it's silly to think like this. We had one night together, which was based more on sentimental nostalgia than anything else. Although the sparks between us were undeniable—and the speed with which she came. Mac was into me, that much is sure. It was intimate and beautiful and maybe—but that could be my brain playing tricks on me—even a bit loving. Maybe a love like ours never fully goes away. Maybe parts of it linger in our hearts forever, like embers that can be stoked into a burning fire again. But I'm getting way ahead of myself. And we still have tonight. Who knows what will happen after dinner. If she gives me the slightest opening, I will make a move.

I have to.

I text back.

> Please wear that red dress again.

I might as well start flirting already.

She answers immediately.

> I'm not sure you can handle it.

She's totally right.

———

"I'm getting a vibe," Alan says. "I'm not one to keep a vibe to myself. Something's messing with the peaceful atmosphere at this table." He pins his gaze on me, then on Mac. "Did you have a fight?" He purses his lips as though it's a foregone conclusion—as though he's solved the mystery of the distressed vibes already.

"No," is all Mac says.

"You saw them on the dance floor last night, babe," Charles reminds Alan. "That did not look like two people fighting to me. On the contrary." He waggles his eyebrows.

"Oh!" Alan's jaw slackens. "Oh," he repeats.

"I'm surprised you remember, Charles," I try to change the subject. "You sure do love a glass of champagne, darling."

"That doesn't mean I lose my eyesight when I've had a few." Charles slants his head, then nods. "Hm."

"What?" Mac asks.

"It's not our business, really." Alan sounds as though a juicy piece of gossip is suddenly the last thing on his mind. "Is it, babe?"

"Absolutely not," Charles confirms.

Right. My turn to see through this silly pantomime. Alan and Charles already know and they're trying to draw us out. I glance over at Mac. She shrugs. Does she no longer care that Alan and Charles know? She's leaving tomorrow so that could very well be the case.

"I mean," Alan says, because he just can't help himself. "If you think I have the emotional intelligence of a snail, go ahead and think so little of me. But I'll have you know I can read a room like no other and, well…"

"I saw *you*." Charles points at Mac. "Go into *her* room." He points at me. "After we went upstairs last night."

"When we called your room this morning, Mac," Alan sounds almost accusatory, "you weren't there."

"None of that means anything," I start to say.

"It's okay, Jamie." Mac puts a hand on my arm and her touch shoots through me like a bolt of lightning. "We're among friends." She draws her lips into a wide smile—her TV smile. Her hand remains on my arm, burning red-hot against my skin. "Jamie and I spent the night together and it was, um, lovely. You probably have a bunch of questions, but we're not going to answer those, because it's private."

My brain is still stuck on Mac calling our night together lovely. I'd call it more something like extraordinary or magnificent, but I won't complain.

"You can quiz Jamie all you want after I've left tomorrow," Mac continues. "But for me, it's private, and I'd appreciate if it didn't leave this table."

"Just so you know, Sandra was speculating when I ran into her earlier," Charles says, "but she's newly married so easily distracted."

"She and Tyrone barely made it out of their room all day." Alan pulls a face, which is funny, because of all the things to frown upon, he picks that.

"We did agree," Charles says, "that if either one of us had married Tyrone yesterday, we wouldn't have let him out of the room all day either." He and Alan giggle like schoolgirls. I chuckle along because it's all a bit silly and funny and awkward.

As dinner progresses, I find myself getting more and more nervous. Every inch of me wants to spend another night with Mac, but I don't know how to go about it. Last night, she was the one who suggested we continue the conversation in her room. She was the one who instigated everything. I still don't feel entitled to make a move on her, so the only choice I have is to wait for a hint. She hasn't dropped any so far, and I've been very attentive to the tiniest of clues. She's put her hand on my arm a few times, but that's it—and it's not enough.

As we settle the bill, a sadness creeps up on me because Mac could also decide that she never wants to see me again. If that's what she wants, I have to respect that. Just like I did after Cherry and I broke up and it dawned on me what a terrible mistake I had made. My first instinct was to get back in touch with Mac and beg for her forgiveness but, by then, it was made perfectly clear to me by anyone I asked for advice that Mac didn't want anything to do with me ever again and I'd better respect that choice.

On the short walk back to the hotel, Alan monopolizes Mac, making sure she has his number, and demanding hers. Her flight tomorrow is early and they're saying goodbye tonight—goodbye for now, Alan keeps on repeating. Lucky him that he can do that. But he didn't tear Mac's heart to pieces. That was all me.

I wait until Mac has hugged Alan and Charles and promised to be in touch soon.

"Do you want to go for a stroll?" I ask her when we're alone.

"Sure." Mac doesn't need an evening gown to look spectacular. She looks even better in shorts and a simple blouse. More like herself. Besides, everything looks good on her. Everything—I catch myself before I get too carried away.

We head to the beach and walk side by side in silence. A million thoughts race through my head and I can't seem to land on one to start the conversation with.

"Let's not go too far," Mac says, after a while. "I have to pack and I leave for the airport at seven tomorrow morning."

"Anything I can do to help?" I say, stupidly. Why is it suddenly so difficult for us to have a simple conversation? Or maybe last night was a fluke and this is how things really are.

"You want to help me pack?"

"Definitely." Too flirty, too quickly? I have no idea what I'm doing anymore. I will desperately need that extra week here without her, just so that my poor brain can recover from seeing her again.

Mac just chuckles in return. "Look, Jamie…" She stops, just like last night, but the vibe is totally different tonight. "Last night was amazing. I think we both agree on that, but… for many reasons, I'm not going to sleep with you again."

It makes total sense, yet it feels like getting the wind knocked out of me. I wait for her to give me all those reasons, or maybe just one, but none follow.

"Of course."

"Just like there were many reasons I never wanted to see you again… after, you know?" She starts walking again, so I follow. "You are…" She pauses. "You meant so much to me. You were everything and I just can't go there again. It's a finished chapter of my life."

"You were everything to me as well." It's probably an unfair thing to say, but this role of martyr doesn't really suit me. I'm quite sick of it, frankly. I'm the one who made the mistake and who was fully responsible for us breaking up. I own that and I paid for my error with years of guilt and Mac's absence from my life.

At least Mac doesn't snicker, or mock me for saying that after what I did—because how can I say something like that after I left her for someone else?

"If you ever change your mind or need anything at all," I say. "I'll be there." I so want to grab her hand, just to feel her skin against mine. "Fresh loaf of sourdough, I'm your girl."

"I only recently started buying your bread again." I can't see her face, but I can hear the smile in her voice. "I had it at someone's house and it was so damn good, I said, fuck it, I'm no longer depriving myself of this bread just to spite Jamie. It was silly, because you never even knew, obviously." She follows up with a nervous chuckle. "That's some damn good bread, Jamie."

"Thanks." If a compliment about my bread is all I can get, I'll happily take it.

Mac stops abruptly. "Shall we go back?" She doesn't wait for my response before turning around.

We didn't walk very far and it doesn't take us long before we're back at the hotel.

"Would you like an escort to your room?" I offer.

Mac shakes her head.

"So, this is it?" Tears prick behind my eyes.

"Maybe. Yeah. I think so."

What about last night? I want to ask. You may claim that I'm not a chapter of your life you want to revisit, but why did you sleep with me then? Why did you make me feel like this? But I don't say any of this. Of course, I don't.

"Can I hug you goodbye?" Mac asks.

In response, I open my arms to her as wide as I can. She steps into my embrace and, instantly, it feels like last night on the dance floor, when we both admitted we didn't want to let go. But I must be the only one feeling that way tonight, because Mac doesn't stay in my embrace for very long. Within seconds, she shakes herself free, and I have no choice but to let her go.

CHAPTER 15
Mac

I sink onto Leila's couch. That too-short weekend in Hawaii, followed by four full days of work are quickly catching up with me. I'm grateful that she has decided to cook me dinner, although I know Leila's also very curious about my reunion with Jamie. What better way to coax all my dirty secrets out of me than with one of her scrumptious Persian dishes.

"Where's Izzy?" I ask.

"Upstate with Jackson and Vivian, pretending she's the world's best godmother."

"You didn't go with them?"

"Izzy and I are not joined at the hip." Leila flashes me a smile and it softens something inside me. I've been on edge since I've come back from Hawaii and, to my great dismay, working more hours isn't helping. She pours me a glass of wine. "No offense, but you look like you need a little pick-me-up."

"I'm exhausted."

Leila gives me a look.

"From work," I say a little too quickly.

"Talk to me." She sits next to me and turns her body toward me. "Tell me everything."

And I do, because seeing Jamie again has shaken me so much more than I care to admit, even to myself. I haven't told anyone about our night together, hoping I could just file it away as something that happened, maybe even convince myself that it was some kind of closure to the most important relationship I've ever had, but flashes of it keep popping up in my mind at the most inopportune times, threatening my TV smile.

"I had so not expected that." Leila's forehead crinkles as she frowns. "I thought you hated Jamie."

"I do. I did. I mean, not really. What is hate, anyway? Does it even exist without a little bit of love?"

Leila huffs out some air. "Are you okay?"

"No." I swallow hard. "Jamie is a box I closed long ago. I had to. But she's still Jamie. She's still all the things I liked about her so much. And fuck, she's so goddamn sexy."

"She must be." Leila has never met Jamie. She knows who she was to me, but I didn't discuss her very often. She's just the elusive ex who broke my heart. "Why else would you sleep with her? Were you drunk?"

I shake my head. "Absolutely not." I've been asking myself the same question since our last hug goodbye, the one I had to break off abruptly in case my body took over from my brain again, my silly subconscious craving for all things Jamie. "I did it because…I wanted to. I wanted to so very badly and, in the moment, I couldn't think of a good enough reason not to kiss her." I let my head fall back dramatically. She's still a damn good kisser, I think, but don't say out loud. "Fuck, Leila." I rub my fingertips against my forehead. "It wasn't just good to be with her. It was special. There's no other word for it. That night was something special."

"Wow." Leila looks puzzled. "And now what?" She hasn't heard many good things about Jamie. To her, Jamie Sullivan might as well be the devil herself.

"She asked if we could see each other again, but I shut it down. I had to. I can't go wherever that may lead. Jamie's the past." She certainly didn't feel like the past when she was in my bed last Saturday. "Part of me wishes I hadn't seen her again."

"I bet other parts of you don't agree with that," Leila jokes.

"It's not like I have an array of lovers to call on for all my sexual needs."

"We talked about this not so long ago. Remember?" Leila peers at me over the rim of her wine glass. "You admitted that you'd basically given up on love."

"What does 'give up' even mean in that context? I stopped looking. Stopped using those disappointing dating apps that never amount to anything. If someone I'm interested in asked me on a date, I would say yes, though."

"The problem is…" Leila twirls her glass between her fingers. "As we also concluded when we had that conversation about love, not a lot of people seem to interest you. You haven't been on a date in forever, and I know it's not because of a lack of interest in you."

"Are you saying I'm the problem?"

"You certainly were when you and I were together." Ouch. Leila's not mincing her words tonight.

"About that…" This is getting a bit heavy for my already weary head. "I spent time with another old friend, a lovely guy called Alan, and according to him you and I weren't meant to be because you were meant to be with Izzy."

"What's his name, you say? Alan? Must be a hell of a guy if he spouts bullshit like that."

"But you and Izzy are so happy. If you and I had stayed together, you—"

"Mac," Leila interrupts me. "What are you talking about? We broke up because you didn't trust me. Because you drove me crazy with all your insecurities and hang-ups. Izzy's got nothing to do with that."

"Yeah, well, Alan would love to meet Izzy. And you," I blurt out.

"Okay." Leila sits there nodding, stunning me.

"What?" I examine her face. Is she all right? Izzy doesn't agree to meet friends of friends just like that, let alone old acquaintances of friends.

"Izzy and I will happily meet this Alan guy, but I want to meet someone in return."

"Really?" I'm not sure what's happening. "Who?"

"Jamie," Leila says. "I'd like to see for myself what she's all about."

"You want to meet Jamie?"

Leila nods. "I do."

"Personally, I don't really care all that much if Alan gets to meet Izzy." I say.

"I'd still like to meet Jamie."

"Why?"

"*Why?* Because even though you broke up twenty years ago, she is the woman who has shaped the course of your life the most. The woman who has made you into the person you have become. The woman you promptly ended up in bed with the second you laid eyes on her again. I think it's high time I met Jamie."

I'd like to think *I'm* the woman who has shaped the course of my life the most. "I just told you I don't want to see her again."

"I guess this is my way of suggesting that you might want to reconsider that." Leila puts her glass to the side. "You slept with her, Mac. I know that's a big deal. You don't sleep around."

"Jamie's not just anyone."

"Obviously." She pats my knee. "Think about it." She grins at me. "You can have us all over for dinner at that swanky penthouse of yours."

"But I hate cooking," I stammer.

"This is New York. You don't have to cook at your own dinner party. There are thousands of caterers." She keeps on grinning. "Argument rejected. Try again."

She's trying to get me to say that I really, really, *really* don't want to see Jamie again, but I can't say that. Leila's right. I did sleep with Jamie, just like that, after all that time.

"It's not the worst idea." I drum my fingertips on the arm rest of the couch. "Don't you have to check with Izzy?"

"I'll text her right now." Leila reaches for her phone. "Actually, I'll call her. I can't explain all this via text." She grins at me.

Leila is the very personification of how Jamie screwed up my life. It was easy enough to fall for her. She's smart, accomplished, and absolutely gorgeous. Her only flaw was that she wasn't Jamie Sullivan. When I met Leila, years had gone by since Jamie left me, and I still couldn't open myself up to her completely. I couldn't fully let her in because what if she left me out of the blue as well? What if we became really serious about our relationship and truly committed to one another, only for her to pull the rug from under my life? These were all very real possibilities and I never managed to exist in a new relationship without that chip on my shoulder. Because if Jamie could do it, the best person I'd ever met, the woman I trusted the most, then so could anyone else.

Leila calls Izzy right in front of me. I try to tune out their loved-up chitchat, but it's not possible. I don't begrudge anyone their luck in romance, nor do I feel sorry for myself that I never found it again. Because Leila does have a point that if I'd really wanted to, I would have found a way to love again. I only had to hear the exact same thing from the therapist I saw every single week throughout my thirties. I'm almost fifty now and the only conclusion I can draw is that Jamie broke something in me that never managed to heal. Whether that's through my own doing or because of the severity of the fracture, I may never know. It's probably a bit of both.

Or, maybe, it's as simple as me never wanting to be with anyone but Jamie. As ludicrous as it sounds, I've entertained the thought more than once. Maybe, for me, there was only one person who could be the love of my life, and I lost her to someone else. But if that were really the case, surely my heart would have started opening up again when Jamie and Cherry broke up. When I heard that she wanted to make amends with me. But instead of jumping for joy, my heart shrank even farther at the prospect of seeing her again.

"Mac." Leila waves at me, her phone pressed against her ear. "You can vouch for this Alan? We only have your word to go on that he isn't some homicidal maniac."

"I can." I only spent a few days with Alan and I can't really vouch for anything, but I knew him years ago, and he's one of Jamie and Sandra's best friends—and I trust their judgements. "He also has a wonderful husband. Charles. You'll love them. They're excellent company." Thank goodness Alan and Charles were at that wedding. I'm not sure how I would have faced Jamie alone. Them meeting Isabel Adler can be my thank-you for being there, for defusing the tension and adding a light note to what otherwise could have been a difficult situation.

Leila and Izzy say their goodbyes. "You've got yourself a deal," Leila says.

"Sounds more like you've got yourself a deal."

"How about we both get something out of it?" Leila rises. "Isn't that the very definition of a deal?" She smiles down at me. "Let's eat. The tahdig will be ready."

CHAPTER 16

Jamie

We were still in Maui when Alan got the text from Mac. His eyes nearly fell out of his head reading it. He had to show his phone screen to Charles several times to reconfirm before he could actually believe it. It was only after he processed the shock that he said, "Oh, and James, you're invited too." Then I had my own shock to process. But here I am, another week later, a bottle of excellent wine in my hand—I considered it too weird to bring a loaf of my own bread— in a cab outside of Mac's building.

"We're here, Ma'am," the cab driver says again.

"Sorry. Yes." I swipe my card to pay, take a deep breath, and get out. My head's all over the place. I should have texted Mac before coming, but I was so afraid that something I said might get my invitation to this soiree rescinded, I decided to stay quiet as a mouse.

Ever since we graduated, Mac and I have been Brooklyn girls. For her daily commute, Mac would be much better off living in Manhattan, but she clearly hasn't been able to leave Brooklyn. Or maybe she did, for a while, and came back. There's so much I don't know. There's so much I didn't get to ask because we spent the little time we had in Maui decidedly not talking—and I wouldn't take back a second of that.

Mac lives in a swanky building with a doorman, who opens the door for me and greets me abundantly, as if I've been a guest of Mac's all my life. He knows my name and calls the elevator for me.

On the ride to the penthouse, I wish I'd arranged with Alan and Charles to arrive together, but there was no talking sensibly to Alan after he received the invitation. I'm nervous enough as it is, but I'm also meeting Isabel Adler tonight and god knows what she'll be like. Although I can safely assume Alan will take up most of her time and attention.

It's ten past seven when the elevator doors open, straight into Mac's penthouse. Someone who is not Mac greets me and escorts me into the living area. I clumsily hand the man the bottle of wine I brought.

Mac hired staff for a six-person dinner party? Another reminder that there's so much I no longer know about her, although I will never forget how much she hated cooking. For a college athlete, she ate the most abominable junk food. Anything worked, as long as she didn't have to prepare it herself. I used to joke that her signature move wasn't dribbling the ball past an opponent, but pushing buttons on the microwave.

I'm all alone in the living room, and my eye is drawn to the view of the Brooklyn Bridge through the window. This place must have cost a fortune. I glance around. Where is everyone? Where is Mac? Did I even come to the right place or did a series of misunderstandings lead me into someone else's home? Then I spot a picture of Mac and her mother, Suzanne, and I know I'm exactly where I need to be.

"Sorry!" Mac waltzes in. "Everyone's late, myself included."

"Alan and Charles are late?" My heart skips a beat at the sight of her. "Hi." Mac's dressed in bright orange pants and a multi-colored top, and although she wears it incredibly well, it's not the colors in her outfit that attract my attention the most. It's the smile on her face and the sparkle in her eye. God, that face.

"Today of all days, Alan managed to break a finger. He didn't want to, but Charles insisted they go to the ER."

"Are you kidding?" Poor Alan.

"He'll be okay and they'll be here in half an hour." Mac takes a breath. "Welcome to my home." She shifts her weight around awkwardly, as though pondering whether to kiss me hello or not. As though we haven't done way more than kiss since we saw each other again. "Good to see you."

It's nice to hear, although I can't help but wonder if she really means it. I guess I wouldn't be here if she hadn't changed her mind about seeing me again. I stop waiting for her move and take a step toward her. "And you." I put my hand on her arm and lean in to kiss her on the cheek. It's all very distant, even a little cold. As though every degree of the heat we shared in Maui stayed firmly on the island.

"Leila and Izzy are always late." She shrugs as though she accepted that fact a long time ago.

"This place is amazing." Since I'm not expecting anything resembling a hug from Mac, I walk to the window to take in the magnificent view.

"Thanks." Mac joins me.

Even though she's standing a few feet away from me, I can feel her energy radiate. I should ask my burning question while we're still alone. I might not get a chance later —and she can hardly kick me out now that I'm here.

"May I ask why you had the change of heart?" I turn to look at her face. "About seeing me again?" I somehow manage to sound calm, but on the inside, I'm anything but.

"I made a deal with Leila and Izzy. Izzy agreed to meet Alan and Charles if they got to meet you," Mac says matter-of-factly.

I don't really know what to make of that, but accept it without further questions. The most important thing is that Mac was easily swayed by her friends to make this happen. Maybe I'll get a chance to ask Leila later exactly how easy—or difficult—that was.

"How was the rest of your vacation?" Mac asks.

"Relaxing." And I couldn't for a minute stop thinking of you, I think. To stay in the same room where we slept together, in the bed where we woke up together. To sit on the balcony where we had breakfast together. It was all a constant reminder of what we had and what we didn't. I turn around. "That's a great picture of you and Suzanne. How is she?"

"Still thinks she's the mayor of her town. Her seventy-fifth birthday is later this year. I'm planning a huge party." Mac smiles when she talks about her mother. "How are Clint and Mandy?"

"There are some health issues, but overall, they're doing okay. They've moved in with Brett. He's taking care of them."

"Really? Your brother is taking care of your parents? That's a plot twist I never saw coming."

"I know. Isn't life funny that way?"

"Hm," is all Mac responds.

What's also funny, or at least a little strange, is that the vibe between Mac and me seems to have gone back to the one we had going on before we slept together—when she told me she didn't care about how I felt and stormed out of my room. But it doesn't match up with me being here. Surely, she wouldn't have invited me against her will just because she struck some sort of deal with Leila and Izzy.

"Champagne?" An actual waiter shows up beside us, carrying a tray with two champagne glasses.

I happily accept one. "I didn't think it was going to be such a fancy affair tonight." I tilt my glass in Mac's direction.

She huffs out some air. "I went a little overboard, as if I'm already trying to make up for any embarrassment Alan might cause with Izzy." She chuckles. She's nervous. "I'm also not very skilled at organizing dinner parties. I prefer to attend rather than host." Some things never change.

"All of that for Alan."

"Obviously, it's not just Alan." Her gaze finds mine, but only for a split second. "It's you as well, Jamie."

Ah. We're both nervous then, just showing it in different ways.

"I'll be on my best behavior. I promise." I shoot her a wink, because I might be nervous, but I'm also here. In Mac's apartment, at her invitation, no matter how it came to be.

"If you bring out extra-charming Jamie, you'll have Leila and Izzy wrapped around your finger in a heartbeat."

I have no time to reflect on that, because Alan and Charles arrive and they're not the type to do so quietly.

———

"Jamie," Leila says after the plates of the main course have been cleared. The food is so fancy, I barely remember what the dish was. "Have you been to the roof?"

"Sorry?" It takes me a moment to realize this isn't some expression I've never heard of.

"There's a terrace on the rooftop. Have you been up there?"

Surely Leila knows this is the first time I've set foot in Mac's apartment, but it must be her way of getting me alone. Maybe she has some pressing questions.

Even though they try to avoid the spotlight, I've seen pictures of her and Isabel, but no picture does Leila Zadeh justice. It doesn't surprise me that a woman like Leila would fall for the likes of Mac—and vice versa, although I prefer not to think about that.

"No, but I'd love to see it."

"Come on."

Alan is deep in conversation with Izzy. They're a match made in heaven. There's no better way to describe it. Although initially a tad aloof, I witnessed Izzy thaw in front of my eyes the more time she spent with Alan. He did say he would rise to the occasion, and he hasn't disappointed. It helps that he's the kind of guy who could have a meaningful conversation with a rock. He always knows what to say and he's excellent company, whether you're Isabel Adler or just a mere mortal like me.

Charles has disappeared somewhere with Mac.

Maybe he's pretending to help Mac in the kitchen so Alan can have some alone time with Izzy. It wouldn't surprise me.

On the way upstairs, in the hallway, there's an enlarged picture of Mac in her college soccer days, in NYU Violets uniform. Her hair was much longer then and it's tied up in a high ponytail. From a distance, it's easy to see her as the All-American wholesome athlete that she was, but when you look a little closer, the real Mac comes through. The asymmetries and scars that give her an edge, the imperfections that make her so irresistible. That's the girl I fell head-over-heels for right there. I have to tear myself away from the picture though, because Leila's way ahead of me.

"It's enlightening to finally be able to put a face to the name," Leila says as we gaze out across the river to the Manhattan skyline. "I love your bread, by the way." She turns to me and sends me a wide smile. "The best sourdough in New York."

"Thank you." It was Mac who advised me, when I just started out, experimenting in our tiny kitchen, to focus on one thing only, and try to become the best at it.

"But I'll be honest." Leila has such a dazzling smile. "I didn't ask you up here to talk about bread, no matter how delicious it is."

"I figured as much." We lean against the railing. We're so high up, it's a little scary. I pull back and look at Leila— and her ultra-charming smile—instead of the depths below.

"I'm very fond of Mac. Always have been." She crosses her arms in front of her chest. Leila's not just charming then. She seems very protective of Mac. "I'd like to say that I know her well, but you're a part of her life, of her past I should say really, she has never allowed me access to."

For obvious reasons, I think, but I get the feeling I'm about to be grilled and I don't want to add oil to the fire.

"Clearly, you did a number on her. I've met the occasional emotionally unavailable woman in my time, but Mac really took the crown." She huffs out some air. "Compared to Mac, even Izzy was an easier nut to crack, and god knows how difficult she was."

I read the biography Leila wrote about Isabel Adler. The details of their romance were not included in the book, but Izzy's struggle with life was.

"And then, Mac comes back from Maui with the news that she slept with you. Color me confused."

"Not just you," I say. "It's very confusing for me as well." I pin my gaze on Leila's. "When we said goodbye in Maui, Mac made it clear she didn't want to see me again, yet here I am."

"It didn't take that much for her to invite you tonight."

I can't help myself. A smile blooms on my face.

"Thank you for making this happen." I pause. "But, um, why did you persuade her to invite me?"

"I was curious. Mac has never been very forthcoming with information about you other than that you left her for another woman three months before your commitment ceremony. It's quite the conversation stopper."

I have no response to that—proving Leila's point.

"But I couldn't believe she slept with you in Maui. What's that all about? It's so unlike her. I guess I wanted to see if you still had some sort of magical hold over her. I wanted to see you together in one room."

"And?" My heart beats in my throat.

"She's been uptight all night, which is also unlike her.

Honestly, when I see you and Mac together, I wouldn't know you two slept together. She's so polite with you, it's almost painful to watch. Because that's not how she is. She probably doesn't know how to act around you. She might be a little all over the place, actually."

"She's not alone," I confess.

"I don't know what Mac wants other than to, at all costs, always protect her fragile little heart. But I do know she's not the type to just sleep with anyone. It stunned me that she slept with you."

I inhale deeply, then slowly let the air escape between my lips. "I hurt her so badly. It's normal that she can't act natural around me, even after all this time. As for her sleeping with me, which she initiated, by the way, because I wouldn't dream of making a move on Mac like that… I'm desperate for it to be something more than it was, although I don't know exactly what it was either. But, um, yeah, I don't know." I'm rambling now. "I don't think Mac knows either. We have all this pain between us and it's still so much bigger, so much more powerful, than the love we had, or the memory of that. But maybe, just for that one night in Maui, Mac let go of her pain."

"Maybe," Leila says.

No wonder I'm babbling. I haven't had a conversation like this about Mac in a long time. Add in all the feelings that being with her have stirred up, it's a miracle I'm able to string a semi-coherent sentence together at all.

"What if you and her had a long overdue conversation? To get it all out into the open?" Leila asks.

"Again, Mac's made it pretty clear she doesn't want to rake up the past."

"Just like she made it clear she didn't want to see you again, yet here you are?" Leila has a point, but she also hasn't. She had to nudge Mac for me to be here. I lost the right to nudge Mac into anything a long time ago. "When it comes to you, Jamie, she's the champion of saying one thing, but wanting—and doing—the opposite."

"I'll, um, do my best," I say, because I would love for Mac and I to have a difficult but necessary conversation. We can't go back in time and say the things we needed to say then, but we can still say something now.

"So will I. For Mac's sake," Leila says, reminding me where her loyalty lies.

CHAPTER 17

Mac

"Do we have to talk about this?" I give Leila a look, but she's either too tipsy to interpret it correctly, or she's willfully ignoring me—both are possible.

"If Izzy can take it, so can you." Leila winks at me. Earlier, she and Jamie disappeared onto the roof for a while. I would love to have been a fly on the wall for that conversation. I'll ask Leila about it the first chance I get, when we're alone.

"I can take it," Izzy confirms. She leans her head against Leila's shoulder for a moment. "It was a real meet-cute moment, very much the opposite of when Leila and I met."

"It was a proper eyes-meeting-in-the-mirror kind of moment," Leila says. "We were in the studio makeup room. I was getting my makeup removed and Mac was getting hers applied. I was already in the chair when she walked in. I knew who she was, and I tried to make eye contact in the mirror. I hadn't expected Mac's gaze to linger like that, though. It was like... eye foreplay."

This happened a long time ago and this story doesn't really mean anything anymore, apart from the fact that Leila is very fond of telling it. I've heard her repeat it so many times over the years, but Jamie's hearing it for the first time, and she's sitting right next to me. Her presence in my home has been unsettling. It's like she doesn't belong here, in the life I made for myself after her.

"You make it sound as though we jumped into bed that very evening, after a couple of glances in the mirror." I shake my head. For some reason, I don't want Jamie to think that I would do that—that I'd hop into bed with someone mere hours after meeting them.

"For the record, we didn't," Leila says. "But I hung around the studio until Mac was done and then I asked her out. The rest is history."

"How long were you together?" Charles asks.

"Who wants more coffee?" I say. Turns out I can't do this. Not with Jamie sitting so close to me, I swear I can feel her body heat. I'm so aware of her, of her every move, that it throws me off. It has thrown me off all night. I might have been able to put our history aside in Maui, because I was far away from home and I was there for Sandra most of all, but Jamie's not my friend. She's not like Alan, whom it's easy enough to welcome back into my life. Alan's entertaining and fun. Jamie just gets under my skin in all the wrong ways.

I get up. "Does anyone need anything from the kitchen?" I've barely lifted a finger all night and the irony's not lost on me that I would now suddenly start acting like the prefect host.

"No thank you, Mac," Alan says. "But every dish you prepared for us was sheer perfection."

I crumble up my napkin and throw it in his direction.

"Aw!" he shouts dramatically. "I'm a gravely injured man." He holds up his hand with the broken pinkie finger.

"I think you'll live, darling," Izzy says to Alan, and he melts into a puddle. "Give me your hand."

Alan offers her his hand. Izzy pretends to kiss the tip of his broken finger.

"There. All better."

This entire evening is so strange. I've enjoyed being witness to Alan meeting his idol, but it would have been less stressful, and more fun, if Jamie hadn't been here. I've tried, but I can't relax around her. I can't sit next to her all evening and pretend we're good. It's not an option, because we're not and we never will be.

It would also be easier if she wasn't so damn attractive. Why does my body still react to her like this? I don't get it. And I don't want to know. Maui was a fluke. A consequence of the circumstances. I managed to pull myself together while I was still there, under the spell of the island. I made my decision. I told her, in all honesty, that I didn't want to see her again. So how come she's sitting in my house less than two weeks later? How did this happen? When did I lose control of my senses again and agree to this?

I'm still standing, looking as ridiculous as I feel. As ridiculous as Jamie made me feel twenty years ago. She didn't just break my heart. She also made a fool of me and of our love, of all the beautiful things we had between us.

"Are you okay, Mac?" Izzy asks. "Do you need me to kiss anything better? Apparently, I'm very good at it."

My foolish heart, I think. All the cracks I managed to smooth over since Jamie left and are now starting to appear again.

"I'm going to get some water." There are two full

bottles of water on the table, but I don't care. I head to the kitchen.

My kitchen is spotless, all evidence of my soiree already erased by the catering company.

"Do you need us to stick around?" the guy in charge asks.

"I think I've got it. Thank you so much." Maybe if my guests see the caterers leave, they'll go home as well, and Jamie can leave my apartment once and for all. I can open all the windows and rid the air of her scent. I can go to sleep and wake up tomorrow pretending she no longer exists again.

I say goodbye to the people who helped me tonight.

"How's that water coming?" Jamie appears in the doorframe.

"It's, um, coming." What is she doing here? Why can't she just leave me alone?

"Are you okay, Mac?"

I shake my head. I'm coming apart at the seams. "No. I'm sorry, but I can't have you here. You're not a part of… this." I look around my spotless kitchen, as though it's the perfect metaphor for the life I built after Jamie, but it's just a kitchen. And my life has never been this clean or pretty.

"I'll go. It's okay. I get it," Jamie says. But instead of leaving, she walks farther into the room. "But Mac, do you think we can talk sometime? Just the two of us?"

"What's there to talk about?" I swallow hard.

"Only twenty years' worth of life."

"I'm not sure I can do that."

"You don't owe me anything, but maybe it will be good for you. Just think about it, please. Any time."

"Good for me?" I blurt out. "Like seeing you again has been good for me? I don't think so."

"Please." Jamie looks at me with those dark eyes of hers. Thank goodness she refrains from sinking her teeth into her bottom lip. I'm so all over the place, I might completely self-sabotage again and ask her to stay instead of leave. That's how scrambled my brain is when I'm with her. I have no clue what I want. I want to both shout at her and kiss her. I want to push her away with all my might and let my hands roam all over her body—preferably naked. This is unbearable, and the only way to make it go away is to not be in the same room as her—and to stand my ground whenever someone suggests we see each other.

"It may not feel like it right now, but maybe it *can* be a good thing. For both of us." Jamie smiles at me and it's the kind of smile that takes over her entire face, as though the sun itself has taken possession of her body and is shining from her very core. "Thank you so much for tonight. It was really, um… something else."

Raucous laughter rises up in the living room. For a few moments there, I forgot I had other guests.

"I'm going now. Good night, Mac."

As she turns around and walks away, it's like someone is clenching a fist around my stomach, squeezing it hard. Like I can't bear the sight of Jamie walking away from me. I take a few breaths and steady myself. I rummage around in the kitchen until Jamie has said her goodbyes, until I hear the elevator doors close behind her. I take another deep breath before I face my remaining guests.

"Did something happen?" Charles asks.

"No. I just…" I can't explain what I'm feeling to them right now.

"Was it too hard to spend time with her?" Alan puts his good hand on my shoulder.

"Yes, it was." Because it wasn't just what happened between Jamie and me. It's also all the things that didn't happen. Most of all, it's the painful reminder that, after her, I wasn't able to make the life for myself that I always wanted. And I don't know if that's because of her or because of me. "Maui was Maui, but to have her in my home…" I bought this place, which is luxurious but would be way too small for the family I've always wanted, as a sort of acceptance. When I turned thirty-eight, and I realized I'd never have children, I relented and bought what is, essentially, a female bachelor pad. "It's too much."

"I'm sorry for pushing you," Leila says.

"You didn't, but to be with her in my home made me feel like such a loser. It made me think of all the things I wanted in my life that I don't have."

"Does that include Jamie?" Alan asks.

"What?" My eyes nearly roll out of my head. But Alan doesn't know what I want. Or maybe he remembers. Jamie and I were always making plans, dreaming out loud of our big family. "No."

"It sounded like it," he says.

I ignore him, because the last thing I want is Jamie back in my life. "When she came into the kitchen just now, she said we should have a frank conversation sometime soon. Can you believe that?"

"That's on me," Leila says. "When we were on the roof, I suggested that."

"This is why I didn't want to see her again. I don't want to deal with all that bullshit again. What would we even talk about? Like I want to know about all the relationships she managed to have these past two decades." At least, she doesn't have kids, I think. It's an ugly thought I regret immediately, because I would never begrudge anyone having kids. On the contrary.

"Mac." Izzy's voice is calm and soft. "You're obviously hurting. Maybe Leila's right. Maybe you should have the conversation you don't want to have and then you can start to feel better again."

"I felt perfectly fine before I went to Sandra's wedding." I might not have had the family I always dreamed of, but I was satisfied with what I did have. My job, my friends, my home. My life was more than adequate until Jamie came along and reminded me of what I really wanted. "I'm sure that, given a little time, and no more encounters with Jamie Sullivan, I'll be right as rain again." Where's the fast-forward button of my life? I'd like to press it really hard, so I no longer have to live with that ache of longing in my gut. That increased pulse between my legs whenever I look at her. How my skin yearns for her touch sometimes because I've also had to resign myself to the fact that no one else can make me feel like Jamie does.

Maybe Izzy and Leila are right. Maybe I need to get Jamie out of my system once and for all. Hurl all the things I've buried deep inside myself at her. Call her unspeakable names for tearing up my heart and my dreams. Make her understand that if I failed at one thing in my life, it wasn't that I didn't manage to keep her, but that I wasn't able to get over her completely.

"Sleep on it," Izzy says, as though I'll be able to sleep at all tonight.

CHAPTER 18

Jamie

Let's talk then.

The message arrived at half past three in the morning. It was the first thing I saw when I woke up and switched on my phone.

It's now four in the afternoon, and Mac is about to arrive at my home. I'm on edge because while we were texting back and forth to arrange our meeting, Mac also wrote that it wasn't going to be pretty. I don't know how to prepare for that—and I'm already so defenseless when it comes to her.

I pace back and forth through the living room, fluffing up pillows, straightening frames on the wall, noticing all kinds of imperfections that I've never paid any attention to before.

Mac's place was flawless—and she used to be so messy. I was the one who insisted on a clean kitchen, especially after one of her disastrous cooking spells. Once in a blue moon, she'd get it in her head to prepare us a meal, her chaotic efforts creating pandemonium in our tiny kitchen.

A shadow crosses the window, but it's just a passerby. There's noise upstairs. My landlady, Miss Carol, is probably puttering around in her kitchen. Unlike Mac, Miss Carol is an excellent cook, and she usually makes a humungous portion of something delicious on a Sunday afternoon, always sharing some of it with me.

Even though I can't really see who's in the street, I know Mac has arrived. I can feel it—it's as if I still have a sixth sense when it comes to her. An instant later, the bell rings. I hurry to the door and brace myself.

There are no pleasantries, let alone a kiss hello. Mac waltzes into the living room like a human tornado. It's only when she's reached the dining table, a natural stopping point, that she takes a second to glance around. She doesn't comment on my interior design choices. It's not why she came.

"Drink?" I ask.

In response, Mac just sighs. "Fuck," she says, after a few seconds pass in silence.

"I'm afraid I don't have that," I joke, because this tension needs to be broken as soon as possible. It hangs too heavy in the air. But it clings to Mac like a second skin and I'm afraid that as long as she's here, things are going to be very fraught.

"I'll take something strong." She shrugs off her coat and tosses it onto the back of a chair.

"Manhattan?" I quirk up an eyebrow. She used to love my Manhattans.

"Sure."

"Still no cherry?" Oh, fuck. I only realize when I say it.

"No," Mac says drily.

"Sorry. That was not an inappropriate joke, I promise."

"It's actually kind of funny." The first hint of relaxation breaks on her face, but it's just a hint, and we have a long way to go.

"I'll be right back. Make yourself comfortable."

The kitchen is at the back of the apartment but not in a separate room, so I can keep an eye on Mac. She walks around, looking around the place. She stops at the wall behind the dining table to look at the pictures hanging on there. Unlike Mac, I never removed all evidence of her existence from my life. I framed a few pictures of our time together. In my view, a decade warrants a couple of photographs.

I mix the ingredients for our drinks. I should be focused on what I'm doing, but I can't keep my eyes off Mac. It's odd to have her in my home, to have her looking at the moments of my life I've chosen to display in my living space. She seems entranced by the picture wall. There are quite a few people on there that she's never met, including pictures of the two women I had a longer relationship with after her. Luckily, there are no pictures of Cherry. I don't need reminding of her.

I can mix a Manhattan in my sleep and it doesn't take long to prepare our drinks. I bring them over to her.

"I can't believe you still have pictures of me on your wall," Mac says.

Since she's here to have an honest conversation, I decide not to mince my words. "We were together for ten years. Of course, I'm going to have pictures of you."

She doesn't question my choice any further. She takes a sip and points at a photo. "Who's that?" In the picture, my arm is slung over another woman's shoulder.

"Shannon."

"Girlfriend?" She takes another sip.

I nod. "We were together for almost four years."

"Really?"

I drink as well. I get a feeling I'm going to need the liquid courage. "Yeah."

"What happened?" Mac turns to me and quizzes me with her eyes.

"It ran its course, I guess."

"Oh, that's right. You called yourself a serial monogamist in Maui. I've been wondering about that."

It was a pretty flippant thing to say at the time—but so was Mac's reaction to it.

"Are you still friends with Shannon?" Mac asks.

"Sort of. We don't see each other every week, but we keep in touch."

"So it wasn't an acrimonious split." She looks away from me and focuses on another picture. "And this? Who's this?"

"Robin. Also an ex." Robin bears a striking resemblance to Mac. I can admit that now, although I refused to at the time when someone dared to point it out to me.

"She's very pretty," Mac says, and I don't know if she means it or if she has also noticed the likeness and is toying with me. "Also ran its course?"

"Robin dumped me."

"And you still have her picture on your wall?"

"She was important to me, so yes."

"Are you still in touch with her?"

"No." Some people, you have to let slip away. Like I had to do with Mac, after Cherry and I broke up and I was desperate to get back in contact with her. And Mac rightfully refused.

"Why did she dump you?" Mac eyes Robin's picture as though trying to unearth some secret from it.

"I guess because she fell out of love with me."

Mac does a double-take, almost as if she can't believe someone would be so stupid as to fall out of love with the likes of me.

"Did she hurt you?" Her gaze lands on me again.

"It tends to be rather painful when someone you love tells you they no longer feel the same."

"You don't have to tell me." Mac's gaze turns into an intense stare.

"I still loved you very much," I blurt out, but I can hardly ask for her sympathy because I was in the impossible situation of loving two women at the same time. Although my love for them was very different. I loved Mac with all my heart and soul. I fell in love with Cherry on a crazy, reckless whim.

"Sure you did." Mac scoffs.

"I did, Mac."

"I know it's not true, because you don't do what you did to someone that you love. You simply don't." She looks away, at the picture of her and me at Rockaway beach, where I asked her to marry me—legally as soon as we were able to, but unofficially as soon as possible. We met Cherry not long after.

"I think you know it's not as black-and-white as that," I say.

"Don't you dare patronize me when it comes to what you did, Jamie. Just… don't."

"I'm not. I'm just saying that leaving you was the hardest thing I ever did in my life. That it wasn't a cut-and-dried decision. That I second-guessed myself every single day. And with good reason, because it also turned out to be the stupidest decision of my life."

"Then why did you do it? Why did you throw it all away? We were so good together and you just... up and left. For *her*."

"I was stupid. Lovestruck. Blind to the consequences."

"Do you have any idea what that feels like? When the woman you love more than anything falls in love with someone else and she wants to be with that other person so badly, she unceremoniously dumps you?"

"No," I say honestly. "I don't know what that feels like, but I imagine it's one of the worst feelings in the world."

"It crushes everything you are. It took me a long time to understand that I wasn't the problem, but you were. I truly believed that I must have done something wrong for you to leave me like that, because I knew you as such an upstanding person with her heart in the right place. A decent woman through-and-through. Someone I could always count on. I trusted you with my life. You took all of that away from me in a flash."

"Of course, I was the problem, Mac. I told you that when I left."

"You think I was listening to that? Do you think I heard anything you said after you told me you were in love with Cherry and you were running off with her?"

We're talking about this as if it happened last month instead of twenty years ago. Maybe this is how it goes when getting closure is too painful—the pain gets stretched out over time and it never gets the chance to go away completely.

"You must know by now how deeply sorry I am about—"

"Why did you and Cherry break up?" Mac cuts me off.

"Because she was a mistake. She made me lose my mind, but when I came back to my senses, I quickly learned that she was the polar opposite of you. She was flaky and unreliable and she didn't have a plan for anything in her life. I couldn't live like that. And I missed you. I missed you so much, Mac. I was grieving for our relationship, for the life we would have had. I was such a goddamn fool."

"You had your midlife crisis twenty years too early."

Is that a joke? It's unexpected but certainly not unheard of with Mac.

"I should have bought a sports car instead."

"You'd already bought that expensive new oven. There was no budget left for a sports car." Mac exhales deeply. She takes a few sips from her Manhattan. "Since seeing you again, I have realized what my biggest problem is."

"What's that?"

"Hard as it is to admit, I never got over you, Jamie." Her eyes fill with tears. "I didn't know how to then, and I never managed to figure it out since." A tear slides down her cheek. "I had time. I had all the time in the goddamn world. And time has helped and healed my wounds, but… I've never been able to get you out of my system completely, which is the main reason why I didn't think we should see each other again. Look at what happened in Maui. Twenty-four hours in the same hotel and I couldn't stop myself from kissing you. What's that all about?" She knocks back the last of her drink and dangles the glass between her fingers. Tears are streaming freely down her cheeks now.

I'm not sure what I should do. I figure just letting her

139

talk is the best thing, to just get her feelings out—although I'd much rather hold her in my arms and kiss those tears away.

"No matter how hard I try, I can't stop thinking about you," Mac says. "About that night in Maui and about all those other countless nights we had together. It feels so wrong, like something I should not be doing. Like I'm betraying myself."

"I can't stop thinking about you either, Mac."

"I want you out of my head so badly, because it's tearing me apart." Mac sniffles and wipes something off her nose. "If I'd known it was going to be like this, I would never have gone to Sandra's wedding." I don't think she heard what I said. Or maybe she just doesn't want to hear it. Maybe it only makes things worse. "Another clock that can't be turned back."

"But, Mac, it doesn't have to be such a bad thing," I whisper. I'm afraid to actually say the words out loud.

"Maybe for you." Her eyes are red and moist. "For me, there's nothing good about it." She looks away, then moves. She puts her empty glass on the dining table. "I can't walk away, but I can't stay either. It's emotional torture." She grips the back of a chair so hard, her knuckles turn white. "That's basically the story of my life since you left. Before that, I knew exactly what I wanted. I wanted to marry you and have four kids. You know that's what I wanted more than anything, more than being a sports reporter, I wanted to be a mother, and I wanted to be your wife. It was so crystal clear to me. But then you fell in love with Cherry and it's not because you suddenly disappeared from my life that I didn't want those things anymore. And I tried, Jamie. I seriously considered getting pregnant on my own, but I couldn't go through with it, because I grew up with a single parent and I didn't want that for my kids. You know my mother. She's strong and amazing and I love her to pieces. She did her very best for me, but I was still always alone as a child. She was always out working and no matter how admirable that is, I'd rather not be a mother than a mother to a child like the one I had to be."

"I know." Mac doesn't have to explain to me why she never became a single mother. I admire her for it because she gave up on her biggest dream, on the dream she'd had since she was a teenager, for the sake of the kid she never had. "I'm so sorry that didn't work out for you."

"I know it's ludicrous to blame you for that, but I did for a long time. Because you fucked up all the plans I had for my thirties."

"I'm sorry." I swore to myself that this wouldn't turn into an endless sorry fest again, but it can't be helped. Because I regret my choices so much, but even more than that, I regret the consequences of my reckless decisions on Mac's life.

CHAPTER 19

Mac

"You being sorry doesn't change anything," I say. "It never did." I wipe away my tears and do a reasonable job of pretending I didn't just cry.

"I know." Jamie finishes her drink. We sure knocked those back. I wonder if there's any booze left in that cocktail shaker. But I didn't come here to get tipsy and reminisce. I came here to have a twenty-year overdue conversation. Although twenty years ago I didn't know how my life after Jamie would turn out. "Shall we sit?" She gestures at the lounge area on the other side of the room. "Do you want another drink?"

"Just some water, please." As Jamie heads to the fridge, I cast one last glance at her picture wall. My gaze lands on a picture of us. We looked so happy. We *were* happy, which made it so hard to understand why she left. It's also the reason I never really got over her. It would have been easier if we hadn't been such a good couple or if we'd had a bunch of unresolved issues going on between us, but our relationship wasn't rocky. It was solid and strong. And then Cherry came along and messed it all up and I had to ask myself the same question over and over again: if some woman could turn up out of the blue and break us up, how strong were we really? Is there even such a thing as an unbreakable bond? Was it all just an illusion? But if it was, why did it hurt so damn much?

I step away from the wall and walk to the lounge. Already exhausted, I sink onto the couch—I didn't get much sleep last night. I kept thinking about all the things I wanted to say to Jamie today but, truth be told, it wasn't just words running through my head. Many times more than I'd like to admit, I thought about Jamie's nipples in my mouth. Her hands on my skin. Her tongue between my legs.

"Here you go." Jamie hands me a glass of water. She takes a seat at the opposite end of the couch.

"I know it's an unfair question but…" My cheeks flush just thinking about it. "What was it like to sleep with Cherry? It must have been absolutely spectacular if you decided to leave me, and our life, after having sex with her?" It's petty and mean, but I also didn't come here to make friends with Jamie again. I'm here for answers to the most difficult questions.

"Mac, come on." Jamie makes a sound somewhere between a scoff and a chuckle. "I don't remember that."

She's copping out. "How can you not remember?" I sure remember what it was like between Jamie and me— glorious, loving, and utterly satisfying. "If it informed the most important decision of your life?"

"What do you want me to say?"

"Just tell me truth. You owe me that."

"I don't want to hurt you all over again."

"You won't hurt me, Jamie. You can't hurt me anymore," I lie.

"I've chosen not to remember and I prefer not to talk about that." Jamie's voice is unexpectedly firm.

"How can we talk about us, about our break-up and the reason for it—about fucking Cherry—if you don't want to tell me what was so damn special about doing it with her?"

"Because it's beside the point."

"The hell it fucking is." I bang my glass of water onto the coffee table with a little more force than I had antici-pated. "It's the point exactly."

"Mac, please, don't torture yourself like that."

Jamie's right. What's the purpose of me either hearing her say how utterly amazing it was to be with Cherry—something I already know—or have her tell me lies. It's just me punishing Jamie, making her pay for what she took from me. It's why I can't bear to be in the same room as her, but I'm here despite that. Despite wanting her to leave my home last night, I came here today. Because there's also the other side of the coin. The reason I can't stand it. Because she's still enchanting to me in some ways. There are still parts of her I want to know, or get to know all over again. There are the times we had, and maybe my memory has played that trick on me where it has painted everything in a soft, pink shade of gentle happiness and I only remember the good times, before the final, ultimate bad spell. And there's the fact that I slept with her in Hawaii—and that it was utterly spectacular to be with Jamie again after all this time.

So, of course I'm here. I'm just not entirely sure what I'm here for. I breathe in deeply and try to calm the nerves tearing through me, that uncomfortable sensation that is the opposite of how I used to feel when I was with Jamie who, for ten amazing years, was my home, my rock, her strong arms always there to catch me.

I glance at Jamie. She was never a glamour-puss. Her jeans often had dough stuck to them, and she never splashed out on expensive clothes because flour gets everywhere when you're a baker. But I vividly remember how she looked in that tuxedo at Sandra's wedding. How well she wore that. How she fitted snugly in my arms when we danced, as though we never stopped dancing together after we broke up. How my body reacted to her touch, as though it remembered everything, and had stored up all the reactions to her touch it was denied for twenty long years.

We might not be very good at talking about the hurt between us, but, that night in Maui, we excelled at other things. It was so much easier to simply surrender to her touch instead of having another painful conversation—to let our bodies do the talking.

Maybe that is the real reason I'm here. Although that's even harder to admit to myself. But all I have to do is look at her. I don't feel disgust when I rake my gaze over Jamie's body. It's not just pain that bubbles to the surface.

It's no wonder I don't want to talk anymore.

"Okay," I say. My throat is swollen from the crying I did earlier. "Maybe I should go." There's no point in me staying if I don't want to talk anymore. I might end up doing something I shouldn't again.

"Mac." Jamie's voice is pleading. "You're here now. Don't go yet. Please."

I can't stay, I want to shout. I'm afraid of what might happen if I stay here any longer.

"It's too much," I mumble. Jamie's too much for me. She was last night and she is now.

"Mac." She shuffles closer to me. "I never got over you either. You've always been the one who got away."

"Fuck that." I shake my head. I'm mostly furious at myself for how I'm letting her get to me.

"We wanted the same things, and I didn't get them either," Jamie says.

It's an open invitation for me to dole out some more blame, but I've done enough of that. It's so easy to see how Jamie hurt herself profoundly as well. I'm not exactly ready to feel sympathy for her in that regard, but I feel a whole lot of other things for her.

"I understand the urge to remove yourself from this situation. It's uncomfortable and painful, but..." She swallows hard. "No matter how many painful memories are dredged up, seeing you again is so worth it. It's so..." Oh fuck. She sucks half of her bottom lip between her teeth. Luckily, she's not done talking, and she lets go. "It somehow feels right. Difficult, but right."

I try to think of something to say, but my brain has had enough of coming up with more sentences. I really am done talking. Although 'right' is the last word I'd use to describe this situation—I've fallen to pieces too many times since seeing Jamie again to be able to call it that. But we're different people. She's not only the Jamie I used to know. She's also a woman I'd like to get to know. Most of all, and I might as well admit it now, she's a woman I'd very much like to kiss. Again.

Her lips on mine are all I can think of. I focus on her mouth. On those exquisite lips. I let my body take over. My most basic urges. The parts of me that still react to Jamie in this way. The parts that never got over her and that I had to push away again and again, but are coming to the fore now. Because I'm sitting in her living room and

147

the distance between us is so small, it would be foolish not to kiss her. I couldn't pull myself away if my life depended on it. I'm so drawn to her, and I've reached the point that I no longer care about the consequences or all the things it could mean. I don't care what it says about me or my self-respect, that I'm about to kiss the woman who hurt me the most. I'm usually not that much of a sucker for punishment—although this doesn't feel like punishment at all.

"Oh, fuck," I mutter under my breath, as I lean in. As I kiss her—again.

When our lips touch, so much of the tension I've been holding in my body simply dissolves. And this, our lips meeting, does feel right—and there's nothing difficult about it whatsoever.

CHAPTER 20
Jamie

Mac's kissing me. It didn't really come out of the blue, but still. Mere minutes ago, she was asking me what sleeping with Cherry was like. My heart goes out to her—in more ways than one. All of this is so confusing. There's so much left unspoken. Earlier, when I looked into Mac's eyes, I could see the pain in them. The pain that I caused her. Yet, she's kissing me and I'm kissing her back. It's all I've wanted since Maui. It's all I've dreamt of. I can hardly blame her for blowing hot and cold. Of sleeping with me one day and never wanting to see me again the next. I have infinite amounts of understanding for Mac.

Over the years, every time I had the urge to get in touch with her, I tried to put myself in her shoes. I imagined how I would have reacted if she had left me for Cherry. How that would have made me feel. How that would have ripped my heart straight out of my chest. Thinking of how Mac must have felt always made me instantly give up on my desire to see her again, because I had no right. When you hurt someone like that, you lose the right to everything forever. Yet, here we are. Just like in Maui, it feels like a miracle. Like life playing the best trick ever on me.

Mac brings her hand to my cheek. Her lips touch against mine again and again, only leaving the briefest of moments to catch our breath. Her tongue slips into my mouth. I pull her close to me. I want her so much. It can't only be the longing I feel for her in this moment. It must be multiplied by all the residual longing—two decades' worth—for her that I never got to express. This is not a run-of-the-mill kiss either. It's magnified by all our history but also by what it means for us today. For Mac to kiss me like this, she must still have feelings for me. She told me that she never really got over me. Although that could mean a number of things, to me, it means that, at the very least, she wants to sleep with me again. Because this is not the kind of kiss that will just fizzle out. It's the kind that's going somewhere.

Mac's hand slides down, finding the hem of my top. She slips her hand underneath, her fingers hot on my skin. I moan into her mouth. I have to rein myself in because what I want to do most of all is get all her clothes off and have my tongue between her legs as quickly as possible. I want to feel her thighs clasp against my cheeks as she comes hard for me. But I must restrain myself. I have to let her take the lead.

Because we're not in Maui anymore. This is no longer the first time we're seeing each other again. This means something different. Something more. And I need Mac to set the pace for whatever this is—and what it might become. Just as I need to give her space to stop this if she wants to, although judging by the intensity of her kiss, and the speed with which her hand slides into my bra, Mac does not want this to stop at all.

Her fingertip brushes against my nipple and I'm starting to lose it already. My body is no longer attuned to her as it was before, but it sure does still respond to her touch. To think that I nearly ruined the afternoon when I claimed earlier that she was the one that got away. I get that Mac can't deal with me saying things like that, but it's the absolute truth. I've known love since we split, but none of the women I loved after Mac felt as though I let them slip from my life too soon, too rashly, too recklessly. Only Mac does.

With our lips still glued together, we maneuver so Mac can unhook my bra. Then we do have to give our lips a break. My sweater and bra get tossed into the room somewhere, then Mac comes for me again.

I sneak a quick glance at her face. Our gazes meet for a split second and it has the same effect as the hottest kiss. I melt under her gaze and I really need to get some of her clothes off now, but she doesn't let me. She opens the button on my jeans and I have no reason to protest. I let her do to me what I so desperately want to do to her. I let her take off all my clothes and push me back onto the couch.

Before she starts kissing me again, Mac hoists her top over her head. There's too much fabric covering her breasts to my liking, but I can hardly complain about that. Then her body is all over mine again and I certainly don't have any complaints. If her being here felt right, albeit difficult, earlier, her body in my arms feels as if the universe is realigning after decades of disarray. Every atom in my body is finding its right place.

I breathe in her scent and it's the most divine smell in

the world. Tears prick behind my eyes, but I don't intend to break down as I did in Maui. Of course, I'm emotional. I loved Mac for much longer than the ten years we were together. I still love her now, although it's a different kind of love. It's wrapped in all the guilt and shame I carried around for years, and that I can finally let go of—some of it, at least.

"Good god," I groan, when Mac wraps her lips around my nipple. I run my hands through her blonde hair. She sucks my nipple deep into her mouth and I'm about ready to explode. I want to give myself to her so badly, so eagerly—as though it can make up for what I did. Mac cups my other breast with her hand and a tiny teardrop escapes my eye. I can't possibly hold back my emotions when Mac is doing this to me. When she is giving me this level of relief—and I haven't even climaxed yet. But so what if I cry? So what if she sees how much she means to me.

Oh fuck. She's moving downward, pushing my legs apart. She kisses my inner thighs and I brace for the divine touch of her tongue on my clit, but she keeps me waiting. Then, instead of giving me the sweet release I'm craving, she crawls back upward. She positions her body next to me and I'm afraid she might tumble off the couch, but she holds on close to me.

"I want to see you," she whispers, sounding out of breath.

Oh, sweet Jesus. If this wasn't actually happening, if I wasn't looking up into Mac's gorgeous blue eyes, I wouldn't be able to believe any of this. Not that she's back in my life and certainly not that she wants to look into my eyes as I come for her.

Her hand dips down. Her fingertips skate along my

thigh, drawing circles, ever closer to where I'm about to explode. It isn't just my desire for Mac I've had to keep bottled up for so many years. I've had to hide my pain more times than I can count, because not many people believed I had a right to it—including myself. I will always be the woman who hurt Mac, but I'm not only that woman. I'm also just a human who made a terrible mistake—the most human of human things to do. I've had to find a way to forgive myself and to live with myself after I left her.

When Mac's finger edges along my clit, it's a hell of a lot more than sexual desire being released. It's the remnants of the existential crisis I had to shepherd myself through. Of having to live with hurting the woman I loved in the most excruciating way.

She keeps staring at me, as though she's looking for something in my eyes that can't be said in words. I've already told her I'm sorry so that can't be it. Unless she needs more apologies—or something more than an apology. Complete surrender in this moment is all I can give her. I try to keep my eyes open because I want to see her as well, but I'm in too much of a state to read anything in Mac's eyes. All I know is her expression is kind and merciful and, just as my eyes fall shut, I'm also convinced that there's something akin to love in her glance.

But I'm on the verge of coming so what do I know? My brain stopped working properly a while ago—when she pushed my naked body onto the couch.

Mac's finger is soft but relentless on my clit. My breath comes out ragged. My body writhes underneath her touch. But again, she doesn't take me there. Instead, she slips two fingers deep inside me, and I feel like I stop breathing altogether for a few seconds.

As I gasp for air, I open my eyes. I peer at her through narrowed eyelids. All I need is the sight of her face, a face that used to be so familiar to me I could locate every freckle blindfolded, for me to quickly be on my way to a climax again. It's been building for a while now. I don't remember Mac playing me so expertly, but there's so much I don't remember. So much falls through the cracks of memory over the course of twenty years.

Mac's no longer holding back. She pushes high inside me and I'm about to lose it. I meet her strokes, bucking against her. If I could, I'd take more of her, but she's already giving me so much. I close my eyes as I ride the first wave that crashes through me. I come at Mac's masterful fingers, because seeing her again isn't just right. I swear it's also meant to be—although she may very much disagree.

CHAPTER 21
Mac

J amie pulls me onto her naked body. She curls her arms tightly around me. Already, I don't know what to do with myself. It feels so different to how it was in Maui. Because we're back home now. We're back to our normal, everyday lives, and Jamie fits into mine like a square peg in a round hole.

"Fuck," she says on a sigh, her lips against my ear. "My god, Mac." At least she's not crying this time around. If she were, I wouldn't be able to do what I'm about to do.

Jamie's fully naked underneath me. Her body is warm and her embrace hard to get out of, but I can't stay. I have to tear myself away from her, from this, as quickly as I can. I have to protect myself. To see her like I've just seen her opens doors inside me I would very much like to remain shut forever.

"I'm sorry, Jamie," I mumble. "I have to go."

"What?" She loosens her grip on me. "Now?" She chuckles as though I've just told her a lame joke. "You can't go now."

"I can and I will." I extract myself from her arms. It's not easy to get out of this couch elegantly.

"Why?" Jamie covers her chest with her arms. She's so naked and vulnerable. Maybe this is how my subconscious does payback, I think, but only for a split second. I don't want to get back at Jamie.

"I changed my mind," I say. No one can argue with that.

"That seems to have become your new specialty." Jamie sits up and reaches for her sweater. She puts it on then looks at me. "What is this, Mac?"

"I can't do this with you. I'm sorry if I gave you the wrong idea." Apparently, it's not closure that I'm after. And my body keeps betraying me when I'm with Jamie. When I catch a glimpse of her too-delicious lips. When she looks at me in a certain way. I can't allow her to be all over me like I was all over her just now. I can't control the outcome, but I need to be in control of everything that I can. Jamie is not one of those things—she never was.

"You just made me come. That *will* put certain ideas into my head," Jamie says matter-of-factly.

"I have to put a stop to this. I can't take it. You're turning my life upside down and I can't have you do that again. I'm sorry." Why am I apologizing? But I did come here. And I did turn into this person who says yes to a conversation one minute, then shuts it down the next. I'm the woman who instigated a kiss with her twice now, but we're not in Maui anymore. I have to accept that seeing Jamie again has shaken me—it always would. And then I have to find a way to move on. I did it once before and it can only be a million times easier this time around.

I don't like myself much right now. I don't like this

person she has turned me into. This is not me. This is not something that I do. I'm either with someone or I'm not.

"I want to see you again, Mac," Jamie says.

"You can't." I look around for my top and quickly put it on. I'm not even sure if what I'm saying is the truth or a lie. I don't know myself anymore. I just want some peace for my battered mind. "Bye." I grab my coat and purse and hurry out of her apartment, before she can make me change my mind.

I walk home trying to make sense of what happened, my self-loathing growing with every step I take. I don't want to be the kind of person she reduces me to. But I also already miss her. It's infuriating and I don't know how to deal with it. Leila can say that all I need is an adult, frank conversation with Jamie and then I'll be able to move on, but she couldn't be more wrong. Because I can't bear to be alone with my thoughts—and that ache of longing in my gut—I call Leila.

"You were wrong," I say after we've exchanged hellos.

"It happens," Leila says in that relaxed way that she has. Leila might be one of my best friends, but there was a time when she was so much more to me. I fell in love with her—I allowed myself to fall for her because it was impossible not to. Until I fucked it up. Until I had to let her go because even though she was decidedly not that traitor Jamie Sullivan, I couldn't stay with her. I couldn't trust her and I drove her insane with my insecurity and baseless jealousy. "What about?" she asks.

I tell her about the past hour of my day.

"Oh, Mac," Leila says, as though that sums it all up. Maybe it does.

"She drives me crazy," I try to summarize. "I have to choose sanity."

"You want her," Leila says. "You can't accept that, which is understandable. But she's only human, Mac. I know she hurt you, but that was a long time ago, and you can't treat another human like that. It's not fair."

"Life was so much easier when I pretended she didn't exist."

"But she does exist and she's back in your life, no matter how hard you try to ignore that. You can't go back to pretending, Mac. Maybe your instinct is to try, but it's not going to work. The genie is out of the bottle. You have to deal with this properly. But you know what? You're a grown-ass woman and you will deal with it. At your core, you are a reasonable and kind person. Things will be shaky for a while, because she has shaken you, but you will find yourself at the other side of this a better person. Or at least a person with less baggage in life, and that's always a good thing, isn't it?"

"You tell Izzy that she's very lucky to have you."

"I tell her every day, but sure, I'll remind her." Leila laughs and sometimes the joyous sound of someone's laughter is all you need to snap you out of an infernal thought loop. It reminds me that there is so much more to my life, and to me, than this reunion with Jamie. "But Mac, do yourself a favor. Acknowledge that Jamie's back in your life and treat her with respect, even though she didn't always treat you like that."

"Okay," I say, before I hang up. It's easy enough to say. Although I have treated her badly, it's not so much respect for Jamie that I lack. It's respect for myself.

A few days go by and all I can think of whenever I have a spare moment, and also when I don't, is Jamie. Her face when I had my fingers inside her. Her simple and refreshingly direct honesty when she said she wanted to see me again. How I've been falling apart since Maui and how I've been taking it out on her by becoming this fickle mess of a person. But I don't know how to be someone else when it comes to this, to her and what we used to be to each other. She has that effect on me now, although it's not a good enough excuse for my behavior.

Most of all, I can't believe I walked out of Jamie's apartment with my body in such a desperate state of arousal. A couple of nights of tossing and turning have yielded the conclusion that I must have been terrified. Utterly frightened of how she might make me feel—and what it would mean.

I also remember Leila's wise words. It's impossible for me to pretend Jamie doesn't exist. Everywhere I go, I think I see her. When I'm on camera, the entire audience might as well be made up of versions of her. When I turn a corner, part of me always hopes she'll be waiting on the other side.

By Friday, I've driven myself to madness and I can't take it anymore. I text her and I tell her the honest truth.

> I can't stop thinking about you.

It takes hours before she responds, but then she does.

> Maybe because we have unfinished business.

She's not even here, yet my cheeks flush, because I know what she means.

> Do you want to come over tonight?

Only if you don't kick me out before I'm ready to go.

> I promise.

As I press send, I wonder if it's a promise I can actually keep. But then I swear to myself that I will. Because of our history, it's easy to assume I don't owe her anything, but I do owe her that, in the here and now, which is where we are living.

Jamie texts back.

Okay

The three dots of doom keep flickering on my screen and I wait and wait for her next message to come through. When it finally does, a flush travels through my entire body.

Shall I bring The Thing?

Jamie is so deliciously audacious. That I would even remember what 'The Thing' is—but of course I do. And that she would just casually ask me like this, after how I left things last weekend. We've only exchanged a few texts but it's as though I'm falling in love with her a little bit just because of them. Because of her.

My fingers are trembling as I answer.

Please do.

I don't just let Jamie in. As soon as she walks through the door, I pin her against it and push myself against her. I kiss her for all the times that I couldn't and all the times that I didn't let myself. I kiss her to make up for being so volatile and capricious—as if that's even possible. And I kiss her for what she brought in her bag. Every cell in my body tingles with anticipation.

"Is it really me you're so happy to see? Or is it The Thing? Full disclosure: it's not actually the original Thing, so to speak; just a more recently acquired substitute." She grins at me and I melt some more.

"You," I say.

"Can I say something first?" She clears her throat.

"Of course." I straighten my clothes and get a hold of myself as much as I can.

"I have endless understanding for how confusing and complicated this is. For how destabilizing it is." She looks me in the eye—she's good at that. "I don't know what this is either, Mac. All I know is that the urge to see you, to be with you, is infinitely bigger than the urge not to. But…" Oh fuck. There go the teeth. Straight into her bottom lip. Does she not remember how it used to drive me crazy? "You're not the only one with feelings. I need you to know that."

"I know." It's hard to return her gaze. I take her hand and fidget with her fingers. "I'm a mess and it's probably going to take me a while to put myself together again, but meanwhile… maybe we can… have some fun." *Have some fun?* What am I even saying? Not that it isn't fun—some of

161

it, at least—but it's a ridiculous proposition to make to Jamie. As if things could ever be casual between us. As if we don't carry the weight of our history on our shoulders.

"We always were big proponents of fun, you and me." Jamie pulls me closer. "Take all the time you need and know that you can always be honest with me."

"Even if being honest means not knowing what I want?"

"I don't think either one of us knows what we want. Maybe we just have to feel things for a while instead of trying to figure stuff out." Jamie caresses my cheek with the back of her fingers. "You are so very special to me, Mac." Her voice is suddenly hoarse, maybe from emotion, or maybe from something else. "I count my lucky stars that I'm standing here with you, even though you haven't even properly invited me in."

"Come on." I pull her forward. I don't take her into the living room but lead us straight into my bedroom instead.

Jamie tosses her bag onto the bed with a wicked grin on her face. "On a scale of 1 to 10, how frisky are you?"

"Twenty-five," I say, without missing a beat.

"Most definitely a number I can work with." She pulls me near and kisses me. There's less urgency in this kiss, more tenderness and passion. It's very much a kiss from someone who thinks of me as incredibly special.

"Where's your bathroom?" Jamie asks after she's kissed me until my knees have gone weak.

"Just through there." My blood beats heavy in my veins as I point to the door.

"I'll be right back." Before she leaves, she leans into me. "Best get a bottle of lube out."

"Um, I don't have any," I admit.

Jamie looks at me as though I've just claimed my building doesn't have running water.

"Let's not get into that now." She chuckles. "Don't worry. I came fully prepared." With that, she disappears into the en suite.

I don't know what to do while I wait for her. Should I get undressed? Get onto the bed at least? Am I sure I don't have a bottle of lube lying around somewhere? And exactly how embarrassing is it that a woman on the cusp of fifty doesn't have lube stashed next to her bed? My mind whirls itself into a tailspin and I end up hovering, doing nothing, breathlessly waiting for Jamie to emerge.

When she does, I sink onto the edge of the bed from sheer lustful emotion. My eyes go wide at the sight of her. In that moment, I realize that she has given me so much already since we've seen each other again. And now, she's giving me this as well. I hold out my hand to her.

While she undresses me, I'm fully aware of The Thing between her legs. It changes the vibe in this room. It changes how I see her and what I want from her. But again, I can't look beyond this evening. Maybe that's the point. Maybe we just take it day by day—climax by climax —and wait for what tomorrow brings. Tomorrow's the last thing on my mind right now, as I pull Jamie onto the bed with me.

The temperature heats up quickly. The Thing presses against my thigh as Jamie kisses me, as her hand cups my breast, her fingers playing with my nipple. It's a complete mystery how she can still have this effect on me. But she was always the best I ever had. The biggest difference is that back in the day, when we made love, I trusted her with my life. Now, I don't trust her as far as I can throw her, but, apparently, it doesn't make a difference to me when we're doing this. It does so all the more outside of the bedroom. I will never trust Jamie again because she has proven herself to be forever untrustworthy. For that reason, we might not ever become friends again, but my body very much prefers to ignore that fact. It reacts to her on a different, far more basic level.

My body can't get enough of her and it's no wonder. It's as though Jamie remembers everything I like. Everything I want. It's why she suggested she bring the toy that juts out between her legs. And if I'm being completely honest, there are hints, in between deep kisses and delightful sighs, that I could possibly trust her again. That I could love her again. That I could let her back in. But then I remember all the reasons why that's not possible and I have to face reality. She can fool me once, but I will never let her do that to me again. I will never give her that opportunity again. I have a black belt in self-protection for that very reason.

Jamie doesn't ask me with words if I'm ready. She just looks at me, scans my face—she reads me. Maybe, with her, and only in these circumstances, I can be the carefree person I was before she irreparably hurt me. Maybe that's what this is.

"Oh, Mac," she says, her voice cracking a little. "You're so… deliciously you." She swallows something out of her throat. I've been too busy dissecting my own emotions to take hers into account—I do know that. What this must do to her. To come here. To walk to my building with The Thing in her bag.

Jamie's vulnerable and incredibly strong at the same time. It's an intoxicating combination. Every cell in my body pulses, is hungry for her. And maybe I do love her a little in this moment. Maybe I never stopped. Maybe we just pressed the pause button—but twenty years is a long time to pause a feeling.

She kisses me again, long and deep, as her hand travels between my legs. She slips her fingers gently inside me and I can't wait for what's to come.

Next thing I know, she maneuvers off me and then squirts lube into her hand. My breath stalls in my throat as I watch her, as I try to process how utterly gorgeous and sexy she is. I don't know if it's sad or beautiful that no one else has ever made me feel how Jamie has.

She makes sure everything's abundantly wet before she takes position. And I want nothing more than to fully surrender to her, to have her take me like this—to have her fuck me. I watch from under my lashes as she guides the toy ever so slowly inside me, as she spreads me wide, for her—only ever for her.

Something happens to me as she slides deeper inside, as she gently starts to thrust. It's not just physical—of course it's not. I can fool myself all I want.

Jamie's inside me, her body writhes against mine and, most deliciously of all, her face hovers right above mine. She looks into my eyes and all I can see, all I choose to see, is how much she cares for me. How much love there still is between us. I may not ever be able to see it again—it may not be possible in any other context—but right now, it's crystal clear to me.

It doesn't take long before I start coming apart at the seams again. I bury my hands in her silky hair as I meet her strokes. I throw my head back so she can kiss my throat—I have no doubt she remembers how that will send me right over the edge. I come hard as she fucks me —as I let her piece some more of the bits of my broken heart back together.

CHAPTER 22

Jamie

"Excellent taste in bread." I devour a piece of sourdough from my own bakery.

"Look at this place." Mac waves her hand about. "Wouldn't you say I have excellent taste in everything?"

"Hm." This place doesn't feel like Mac at all—not like the Mac I used to know, anyway. "Sure."

If my lack of enthusiasm for her glitzy decor irks her, she doesn't show it. Maybe she doesn't care what I think. At least she hasn't kicked me out yet.

I can tell she's mulling something over. I hope it's not a repeat of the question she asked me when she came over to my place last week.

"Just spit it out." When I look at her, a smile blooms on my face, regardless of which difficult question she may throw at me. Mac looks magnificent in the morning light. Her eyes are bluer than I remember even though I don't know how that's possible.

"I've been wondering if twenty years of hindsight have given you any new insight into why, um, you left me. If there was some other subconscious reason that you could only know afterward."

There aren't any easy questions with Mac, that's for sure. Although this one I've pondered plenty of times myself, because I so wish there had been another reason for leaving her other than my stupid, love-drug-addled brain. Maybe then it wouldn't have hurt so much.

I shake my head. "No."

"It was really just Cherry and all her charms?" It's impossible for Mac to say Cherry's name without it sounding like the vilest curse word. "I didn't inadvertently push you into things you didn't really want? You could have had a family without me, for instance, but you didn't."

"It took me quite some time to get my act together after you. Before I knew it, my thirties were over."

"You could still have had kids in your forties," Mac says.

"But I didn't. It was never the right time and…" The truth is that I never wanted kids with anyone other than Mac. My dream was always to raise tiny humans alongside her. Her enthusiasm infected me and her dreams easily became mine, but they were also inextricably linked with her. "It never happened."

"Can you imagine a little version of you? A little boy with bangs like yours." Mac chuckles.

"How about a mini you?" Even though it's not real, the potential adorableness is almost impossible to bear.

"Sometimes I sit in this chair, in my swanky bachelorette pad, and think about the four kids I wanted. Not often, but sometimes my mind can't help but go there, you know?"

The sudden sadness in Mac's voice breaks my heart. "I'm sorry." There's nothing else I can say.

"It's not your fault. I have to accept that. I could have had kids. I could have done it on my own, but I didn't have the guts... At the time, I just really wanted someone by my side for it, which is understandable, although I do regret it sometimes. Look at my mom. She did it all on her own and I turned out not too bad." She scoffs. "If I'd had a kid by myself, she would have moved to the city to help me, but I didn't want her to do that. She's already done so much for me."

"My dad didn't speak to me for an entire month after I left you," I say, now that we're on the subject of parents.

"I know. For weeks, he called me every other day to check on me."

"He was absolutely livid. And rightly so."

"Still, he's your dad. He should have taken your side."

"Nobody took my side, Mac. Not even my parents. No one."

"Well, you had Cherry."

"My dad would be over the moon to see you again," I say, because I don't want to talk about Cherry. "My mom as well."

"Have you told them that we've seen each other?"

"They knew you'd be at Sandra's wedding so, yes. Did you speak to your mom about me?"

"We're still very close. I tell her almost everything, so yeah."

"When you say 'almost everything...'" I pry.

"I didn't tell her we slept together. Some things, she doesn't have to know." Mac sends me a smile. "My mom always really liked you. She was devastated when we broke

169

up. She was there for me but, sometimes, when I could see beyond the self-pity I was wallowing in, I could tell it really hurt her to see me like that. But you know my mom. She's been single most of her life and her dream for me has only ever been that I'm happy with what I have. Not that I was in a stable relationship and had a bunch of kids. And I have been happy." Mac manages another smile. "That's what my mom told me as well. It's not because your dreams don't come true that you can't be happy or satisfied or fulfilled. So many things can make your life good, and I have a good life. I really do."

"I'm glad." I could sit here for hours with Mac. Looking at her and catching up. Maybe end up back in bed. "What are you doing today?"

"Working," she says matter-of-factly. "If you want to see me tonight, you'll have to switch on your television."

"How about if I want to see you in the flesh?"

Mac shrugs. "I guess I owe you one booty call."

I burst into a chuckle. "I can just call you whenever and you'll come over?"

"That's usually how it works." She grins at me.

"What if I'd like to make you dinner as well?"

"I have to eat, but… as long as it's not a date. I'm not going to date you, Jamie. I need to get you out of my system somehow and, apparently, that somehow is amazing sex, but I can't offer you more than that."

"I guess I can live with amazing sex."

"It's a hard life." Mac extends her hand. I take it in mine.

"Keep your phone switched on at all times," I say as I gaze into her dreamy eyes. "I'm going to cash in on that booty call real soon."

In the next few weeks, one booty calls turns into multiple nights of amazing sex. All we manage apart from that is a few quick meals together. Mac is a busy woman and I have a business to run too. Although, if it were solely up to me, we'd have lunch in a public place once in a while, so she didn't start kissing me every time the conversation goes down a path she doesn't want it to go down. When Mac's gaze lingers on my lips for more than a few moments, I know what she wants. And it's hardly something I can deny her—or that I can resist. But as time goes by, I want so much more of her than what she's willing to give. But I have no choice but to bide my time. There's no point in rushing, or pushing her—it would only have the opposite effect.

CHAPTER 23

Mac

"Hey, Gabby." Lisette, the striking new producer we poached from a rival network, knocks on my dressing room door. "Do you have a minute?" Her teeth are so white, they almost blind me when she smiles.

"Sure." I'm dying to get to Jamie's after a long day, but it's important to keep the new producer happy.

Lisette walks in and closes the door behind her. "I don't know if you know this, but one of the reasons—well, the main reason, really, if I'm being totally honest—that I came to work here is you."

"Thank you so much, Lisette. We're so lucky to have you." I send her my widest smile.

She shuffles her weight around. "Would you be up to grabbing a coffee sometime?"

"Of course. Any time."

"Or, um, a drink after work? Dinner, maybe, if you feel like it?"

Oh. Is she asking me out? My head's been so full of

Jamie, I've been completely oblivious to anyone flirting with me. I don't immediately know what to say.

"Oh, god," Lisette fills the silence. "Did I get this so wrong?" She grimaces. "I've been told you're single and…"

"I am single, I just…" I don't feel particularly single, which is a problem, I now see. I certainly wouldn't ask anyone on a date if I knew they were in a situation like I'm in with Jamie. We're not dating, but we see each other all the time. So much, in fact, that I have to wonder if we aren't dating and whether I'm just being stubborn for the sake of it—which wouldn't be a first. "I'm sorry. I'm in a complicated situation with someone. An ex. It wouldn't be very fair on you to…" *Damn it, Jamie.* "I can't go out with you, Lisette. I'm sorry. It's not you."

"Yeah. Of course." She locks her gaze on me for a split second. "I had to ask." Lisette seems to take it in her stride. She even winks at me. Before she exits, she turns to me. "If your situation changes and you feel like it, I'm game."

I stare at the closed door for a few moments. Maybe Jamie and I need to have a conversation but it's one I'm reluctant to have. I meant it when I said I don't want to date her—at least not officially. There's no point. The part of me that can remain rational around her, which isn't a big part, yet one I rely on heavily, won't let me.

When I arrive at Jamie's, instead of instigating a proper conversation, I ask her a question that's been on my mind since the first time I came to her place, but is yet another thing we have failed to discuss—because we don't do a lot of talking.

"Why are you still renting?" I met her landlady and upstairs neighbor Miss Carol last weekend, when she dropped off a portion of lasagna for Jamie. We ate it together and it was absolutely scrumptious.

"I like to move around," Jamie says.

"How long have you lived here?"

"A few years."

"Is it because you're a serial monogamist? Are you like that with apartments as well? You get tired of them after a while?" I'm pushing it—possibly even angling for an argument because of how Lisette made me feel.

"What's going on?" Jamie and I might not be dating, and she lets me get away with stuff because of it, but she's not going to let this fly.

"I was just wondering if you're seeing other people. If you're looking for the next person to be monogamous with." I shake my head, telling myself off. "I'm sorry. I'm being a bitch and I know it."

"For the record, I'm not seeing anyone else. But I think you know that."

I heave a sigh. "A co-worker asked me out earlier."

"Someone asked you out?" Jamie's eyes widen. Was that a crack in her voice?

"I said no, but…" But what the hell are we doing?

"*But?*" Jamie stops what she's doing.

"I don't know. It was a strange moment. It made me think."

"Did you want to say yes?" When Jamie arches up her eyebrows, they disappear all the way underneath her fringe.

"No, Jamie. Of course not. It just made me question

175

what we're doing, you and I. What I'm keeping you from saying yes to."

"Me?" She puts down the bottle of wine she was about to open. "I'm not interested in saying yes to anything that doesn't involve you. I think you know that, too."

"Come here." I open my arms to her, expecting Jamie to throw herself at me again, as she usually does, but she doesn't.

She leans against the kitchen counter, grabbing hold of it with her hands. "At the risk of upsetting the precarious balance of whatever it is we have, or what you're telling yourself we have…" Her gaze on me is unwavering. "I wasn't going to do this, but now I suddenly feel like I have to." Jamie huffs out some air. "I'm not just falling in love with you all over again, Mac. I'm already head over heels in love with you. I want to be with you. Properly. That you don't want the same is starting to hurt me more and more. What we do have between us, what you're willing to give, is no longer enough. I want so much more. I want to take you out. I want to hang out with you and ask you all the questions you don't allow me to ask because you always have somewhere to be other than with me. Unless it's for sex." Her big eyes go moist. "I'm not sure how much longer I can do this, to be honest."

There it is. The conversation I didn't want to have, because I knew what the consequences would be. What Jamie is saying is hardly a surprise. I feel myself falling too. I am falling, but the difference between us is that I can stop myself, because I have no choice. I can rationalize myself out of it because I know what she's capable of, and that will always stand in the way of me falling for her completely.

"I'm sorry I can't give you more." I can barely look at her, at the hurt in her eyes because she knows what's coming. "It's my bad for letting this drag on so long because I've always known it couldn't be more than this." She can't blame me for not being honest with her about that.

"Can you honestly stand here, look me in the eye, and tell me you're not in love with me?"

"Why does it even matter?"

"It matters a great deal."

"Even if I were crazy in love with you, we still couldn't be together."

"But Mac, don't you see? We already are."

"We're not," I insist. "There's a huge difference between what you just said you wanted and what we have."

"Agreed, but the only thing standing between what we have and what I want to have, is you."

"Well, yeah. I know. But I can't change how I feel about you. I can never trust you again, Jamie. You hurt me too much for that. You broke something inside of me. Something that can't be fixed."

"Maybe you don't want it to be fixed."

"Don't say that, please." Tears well behind my eyes.

"I have to say something. Someone has to." She draws a breath. "I know that nothing I say can make you change your mind. That something inside of you will have to change, but, Mac, come on... we've been so intimate. So close. We could have something so beautiful and you're going to walk away because you're scared?" Jamie shakes her head. "Won't you at least try?"

"Scared?" I quickly wipe away a wayward tear. "Put

yourself in my shoes and see how utterly petrified you'd be."

I may have put a piece of my heart on the line already, letting her into my life again, but I can't give it all to her—not again.

"I know, Mac, but I can't change the past. It happened. It can't be undone. But *I* have changed." She brings a hand to her chest. "I hurt myself as well and there's no way I would ever do that to you or myself again. There's just no way. Can't you see that?"

"No." My breath's becoming ragged. "No fucking way can I see that, and you know why? Because when you left me, you were you. You were the most you that you could be. You were not a different person than you are now. You made the decision to throw me out with the trash once, even though you loved me. Even though you were going to marry me. Even though you knew full well what the consequences would be. If falling in love with another woman can do that to you once, it can do that to you again. That's who you are. That's why you don't commit. You can't. I'm not going to be serially monogamous with you for a few years only to have you break my heart all over again. That's not going to happen."

"If you really believe that about me, what are you even doing here?" Tears stream down Jamie's face and, as it turns out, my heart's already breaking just looking at her like that.

"I can't stay away from you," I whisper. I'm not sure Jamie heard me.

"I'm going to *need* you to stay away from me from now on." I guess she did hear me. "I can't do this with you, Mac. You mean too much to me. It's ripping me apart."

"Fair enough," I stammer. This was inevitable. I

should be getting up and ready to leave, but my ass seems glued to the chair I'm sitting on. My body doesn't want to leave Jamie. I don't want to leave Jamie, but I can't be what she wants me to be and she can't be what I want her to be. Her request makes perfect sense, yet it will be excruciatingly hard to honor. But I've done hard things before. I had her walk away from me before. If I need to be the one doing the walking this time around, then so be it. I'll do it. "I'm sorry. I—" I'm not sure what I could have done differently, except not attend Sandra's wedding. "I'm sorry it has to be this way." Once I do get up, I make for the door immediately, but I can't just leave Jamie like that. I need to feel her body against mine one last time. I need her arms around me.

"Damn you, Mac," she whispers in my ear as she holds me, as I fit into her embrace so snugly, so perfectly, you'd think her arms were made for the sole purpose of hugging me. "I fucking love you," Jamie says.

But I still have to walk away.

CHAPTER 24
Jamie

"I 'll talk to her." Alan has come over to my place. "Talk some sense into her."

"Don't. Please. The sooner I give up all hope, the better." I had no idea it would hurt so much, as if I've gone back in time and made the worst mistake of my life all over again.

"But she loves you," Charles says, as though that's all it takes.

"It's not enough." I had to protect myself. As soon as Mac told me her co-worker had asked her out, my stomach caved in on itself, and I knew I couldn't spend my days pining for more of her—for all the things she wasn't able to give.

"Since when?" Alan is outraged.

"Since I left her three months before our commitment ceremony."

"Yeah. Okay." Even Alan can't argue with that. "But that was twenty years ago." Turns out he can. "This is now." He squeezes my hand. "I get why you can't be the one to talk some sense into her. You're the reason why she's like this. But maybe I can. I can at least try."

"Mac is more than old enough to make her own decisions."

"What are we going to do to cheer you up?" Charles changes tack and even though it's sweet of him to try, I can't be cheered up right now. Maybe this is exactly what I deserve after what I did to Mac. Maybe my comeuppance is twenty years late, but it is finally here in full force.

"I'm going to have to ride this out." You'd think this emptiness inside me would subdue my feelings, but it's the opposite. It's like an echo chamber for every regret I've ever had. For all the stupid mistakes I've made and all the reasons I can't be forgiven for them. And some things are unforgivable—like what I did to Mac.

But why couldn't she have frozen me out in Maui? It might have hurt for that weekend, but at least then it would all have stopped. I might have thought about her once in a while, the way I've done the past two decades, but she wouldn't have dominated my life from dawn to dusk—and all the hours I lay awake in between. It's too late to protect my heart. It has already been broken—again—and I can hardly blame Mac for that.

It's been three days since she walked out of my apartment, and I've wanted to text her every hour since. Every minute. I have no idea how I'm going to get over her, and it serves me right, because while this is painful, it's not half as painful as your fiancée abruptly leaving you for another woman mere months before your wedding. Months before our first IVF appointment. Months before the next stage of our life was about to fully take flight. I don't deserve Mac's forgiveness. I don't deserve her.

My phone buzzes, and my heart skips a beat. Maybe Mac's changed her mind. Maybe she misses me so much, she wants to try after all. Or maybe she decided to cash in one last booty call because, damn it, it was so good between us, and she wants one final taste before she gives it up forever.

I check my phone. "It's Sandra," I say on a sigh. Damn her and her romantic destination wedding. For wanting us both there. But none of this is Sandra's fault either.

"I heard," Sandra says. "About you and Mac and what you've been up to behind my back. How are you?"

I swallow hard. "What did Mac tell you?"

"That you've been sleeping together since my wedding. Why didn't you tell me?"

"Because it was…"

"I get it," Sandra says, cutting me off. "But, Jamie. This is big. Or was big. How can we fix this?"

"It can't be fixed. You should know that if you spoke to Mac in the last couple of days."

"I understand her trepidations, but I told her that she should give you another chance, Jamie. She'll never know what she's missing out on if she doesn't."

"She won't. She can't. I screwed her up too badly."

"People are resilient," Sandra says. "We get over stuff. That's what we do."

"Not Mac. Not over this."

"Is that why she jumped into bed with you the first chance she got?"

"You don't have to convince me, San."

"I have to convince both of you. Mac to not be so stubborn and you to fight for her, damn it."

"Fight for her? How am I going to do that?"

"You'll figure it out. If it's meant to be, it's meant to be." Is she hearing herself?

"You just got married. You might be seeing the world in too romantic a light."

"The hell I am. All I want is for you and Mac to see what you could have. That what I have with Tyrone is possible for the two of you."

"Did you tell Mac that?"

"She's not very receptive to messages like that."

"And I am?"

"Don't give up on her now, Jamie. That's all I'm saying. You gave up on her before and you can't expect Mac to reach out to you. That has to come from you."

"I've been reaching out to her for weeks. I've made it clear how I feel. I can't do more than I already have. I have to protect myself."

"Bullshit. What's the difference now, anyway?" She pauses. "Actually, if you can't see that, then maybe you shouldn't fight for her. Protecting yourself should not be your priority now. You need to go all out for Mac. You need to show her that you have a future together and that you're not afraid, even though she is."

"Are you kidding me?"

"Absolutely not. Mac told me what you said. That you want more than she can give you. That you're bailing. Again. What is she supposed to do with that? Is she supposed to pursue you now? That's not how this is going to work."

"I don't think she told you everything."

"She doesn't have to tell me everything." There's a sigh on the other end of the line. "I know I'm giving you tough love. That's why I wanted to do this over the phone.

I'm not sure I could say these things to your face, to be honest, but that doesn't make them less true."

"But, San, I don't—"

She cuts me off again. "I'm the only one who has had a front-row seat to both of your lives for the last twenty years. I'm the only one who has always been there for the both of you. At the very least, you owe it to me to listen and to take what I say seriously. If you love her, do something. Do more than what you've been doing. Be more patient. Go out on a limb. Fucking fight for your girl, Jamie."

I take a deep breath. I wasn't expecting a lecture, and I have no earthly idea how to go about anything that Sandra is suggesting, but it does offer a glimpse of hope. A different perspective.

"Okay," I say. "I'll try."

"Keep me in the loop, please. You hooked up at my wedding and I didn't even know about it."

"How's married life?" I ask.

"It's fucking fantastic. I can only recommend it." Her voice sounds completely different than before—drenched in love instead of reprimands.

After I've hung up, Alan and Charles are all over me.

"Sandra's utterly convinced I should fight for Mac." One thing in particular she said reverberates in my head. "She can't believe I bailed on Mac again."

"You didn't bail on her, darling," Alan is quick to say. "It's not the same. You have rights here, too. You have feelings, too. Nothing superhuman is required of you. Besides, you told Mac how you feel about her. You told her what you wanted and she's the one who can't give it to you. I don't believe in totally sacrificing yourself for the sake of love."

"It kind of made sense when Sandra said it," I admit.

"Maybe she wanted to hit a nerve so you would do something. So you don't just sit back and accept that it's all over between you and Mac," Charles offers.

"This is why I should talk to Mac," Alan says. "Feel her out. Find out what she really wants." He puts his hand on mine. "But I'll only meddle with your blessing."

"Do it," I say, because that chat with Sandra made me change my mind about giving up hope. "Please."

"I'm on it, darling." Alan squeezes my hand. "Meanwhile, start thinking of ways you can win her back."

I huff out some air. "How do you win someone back who can't trust you?"

"You'll find a way," Alan echoes Sandra's words.

Yeah right.

CHAPTER 25
Mac

"How did you feel when you were with Jamie?" Leila asks. "Not in the moments of doubt, but when you were intimate. When she was lying in your arms."

"I don't want to think about that anymore." Truth be told, I was expecting a touch more understanding from my friend, not this unpleasant interrogation she's subjecting me to.

"You should, Mac. Trust me."

"It was always a confusing mix of emotions," I lie, because when I was in bed with Jamie, for brief pockets of time, I could forget about our past. When I looked into her eyes while we were making love, I could forget she ever hurt me. When she pushed inside of me, I wanted to keep her in my bed forever. "Our past was always hanging over us."

"I have trouble believing that because if that were really the case, you wouldn't have kept sleeping with her for so long."

"Fine. On very rare occasions, it made my heart sing."

My poor old heart that she bruised black and blue. "Every so often, when I was with Jamie, it felt like my soul found some new sparkle again. An effervescence that I haven't felt since she left me."

"That's what I thought," Leila says. She tops up our wine glasses. "Don't you want more of that?"

"That only happened when we were in bed together. It made her extra hard to resist, because who wouldn't want to feel that again?"

"The way I see it." Leila pins her gaze on me. "Is that perhaps instead of just your legs, you should also open your heart a bit more to Jamie."

"Excuse me?" My eyes widen. "Did you really just say that?"

Leila just shrugs, as though she just imparted the world's greatest wisdom.

"For the record, I've stopped, um, opening my legs to her."

"How foolish is that? Do you know how rare it is what you and Jamie have? To feel that way about another person? And you're walking away from that?" Leila shakes her head. "Just because you can't get over yourself?"

"People have walked away from a great love for far lesser reasons."

"I know what I'm talking about, Mac. I never believed in all that bullshit about 'the one' and whatnot. About this person who comes along and sets the world as you know it on fire. In fact, even saying it now, speaking these words out loud, makes me cringe a little, but I can't ignore that it happened to me when I met Izzy. After the past few weeks, there's no doubt in my mind that Jamie is that person for you."

I somehow manage not to roll my eyes. "Being 'the

one' clearly doesn't mean she can't break my heart. And it most certainly doesn't absolve her from hurting me."

"She made a mistake. An enormous one, granted. But you're both here, your hearts and your love relatively intact. You have something to work with, but only if you want to."

"I don't remember asking you here for a lecture." I arch my eyebrows. "I was hoping for a good bottle of wine, commiseration, and bottomless understanding."

"I understand where you're coming from—that place of hurt that still has such a hold on you—but Jamie's not just anyone."

"You weren't just anyone when we were together." I must be desperate if I'm raking up our sad old love story. "You were a completely trustworthy person, yet I didn't manage to trust you and I screwed up our relationship. If I can't trust someone like you, how can I possibly trust Jamie? Who has already proven to me how untrustworthy she is?"

"Was, Mac. *Was.* That was twenty years ago."

"There's no statute of limitations on betrayal."

"Okay." Leila holds her palms up, as though accepting defeat. "If that's how you feel, that's how you feel. I can only tell you what I've witnessed since she's come back in your life."

"Don't you think I've asked myself all of this over and over again? Because I have and I've driven myself mad in the process. Yes, I still love her, or I've fallen in love with her again. I'm insanely attracted to her, and I think Jamie is one of the most magnificent people I know, but I can't bring myself to do it. To take that leap. I simply can't. I don't know how."

"So you admit that you want to?"

"Oh, please, don't pull the semantics card on me now, Leila. The bottom line is she hurt me too much. We can sit here all night and try to discern the definition of 'too much', but all I can tell you is how I feel. I will not put my trust in Jamie Sullivan ever again."

"Okay." She lifts her glass. "I'll be your heartbreak drinking buddy then."

"Thank you." I wonder what Jamie's doing now. Does she have a heartbreak drinking buddy? I'm sure she has plenty. I take a sip of wine. It's going to take a lot more sips to forget about my heartache for tonight. I'd best get to it.

***

"Where were you twenty years ago, Alan?" It's hardly a fair question—and I'm beginning to realize my mind's a bit stuck on what happened then. "When I needed you to advocate for me with Jamie?" As if I could have just moved on after Jamie told me she slept with Cherry. But she didn't just tell me—she also left me.

"I did, Mac. I swear to you. For weeks on end, it's all I did."

"Oh." I don't remember. All I remember, really, is the blinding pain. Pain I didn't think possible on a purely mental level. "Well, whatever you said to her then, clearly didn't work."

"I'm sorry, Mac. For not trying harder and also for losing touch with you. I'm really sorry about that."

"No, I'm sorry for saying that. It wasn't up to you to salvage my relationship with Jamie." *Jamie. Jamie. Jamie.* How is it possible that, twenty years down the line, my life is, once again, revolving around her?

"But still. I should have been there for you more." Alan's very subdued today, almost solemn and not like himself at all.

"I'll tell you the same thing I told Leila. Yes, I have feelings for Jamie. In fact, seeing her again has turned my world upside down, but I don't know how to trust her. I don't know how to get over the essence of what she did to me. She betrayed our love. She made a mockery of everything we had, and we had so much."

"She did. There's no doubt Jamie did that. She was a fool and she'll be the first to tell you that. But twenty years is a long time."

"That may be so, but I can't change how I feel."

Alan looks me in the eye. "God, I've really missed you. All this time not seeing you. It really has been my loss and I'm so happy you're back in my life."

"Likewise." Even when he's being serious, Alan has the kind of face that cheers you up instantly. "I'm so happy for you and Charles." My own heartache doesn't prevent me from being happy for a long-lost friend's romantic happiness. "He's such a sweet guy."

"Charles and I are ridiculously happy now, but it wasn't always like this." Alan tilts his head. "For me, it was… boom! Love at first sight. Not so much for him, though. He strung me along in the beginning."

"He did?" I can't imagine Charles behaving like that. Then again, people behave in all sorts of ways we don't expect them to.

"Oh, yeah. I mean, he is a catch."

"So are you, darling. And clearly, he saw the error of his ways."

"My point is, that love doesn't exist without pain.

There's always going to be something, big or small. But you're the one who decides if it's worth it."

"I can't take that risk."

"Why not? What's the worst that can happen?"

I scoff. "That she leaves me again, obviously."

"Sure, but you know what? That's the same for every other person in a relationship."

"No way. It's not the same. Are you afraid Charles is going to meet another guy and leave you for him?"

"It's not my most pressing concern, but—"

"Of course, it's not, because that would be unbearable, and you trust Charles. You have good reason to. He didn't leave you three months before your wedding."

Alan sighs. I understand. I'm getting tired of the same old song and dance as well.

"You have to let that go, Mac. For your own sake. You have to find a way."

"It's not that I don't want to." Oh fuck. Here come the waterworks. "Jamie…she's…" Trying not to think of her has been impossible. I see her everywhere. "I've never met anyone who even came close to her." I let the tears stream freely. "To be with her again, for a minute there, was like the best dream ever."

Alan scoots closer and holds my hand.

"But that's all it was in the end. All it could be. A dream."

"She loves you, Mac. More than anything. That's all I know."

"This is not about love. She loved me then as well."

"Can we make a deal?" He gives my hand a squeeze.

"Sure," I manage to say in between sniffles.

"For as long as I'm here, you're not allowed to refer to the past, to what happened twenty years ago. I'm not invalidating it, or your pain, but just try, Mac. Try living in the here and now for once."

"That's easy for you to say."

Alan shrugs. "Sure, but still. Give it a try. See how it makes you feel to not always have to relive that hurt again. It might surprise you."

"Another thing I don't know how to do."

"You start with minute by minute," Alan says. "Then hour by hour. Eventually, day by day. That's how it works." He grips my hand tightly again. "Imagine if you and Jamie didn't have history and you'd met her at Sandra's wedding for the first time."

"I would never have slept with her," I blurt out.

"Your loss, I'm sure." Alan tries to hide his chuckle, but he doesn't really succeed.

"Oh, Alan, you have no idea how good it is with her. With Jamie. That night in Maui." I shake my head, because even though I was there, and we've been together many times since, all of them equally incredible, I can't quite believe it either. "What hurts me the most is that we're so damn good together."

"Maybe in your own personal universe there's a law that says it can no longer be like that, but out here in the real world, Mac, there are no such laws. If it feels so good, you're the fool for denying yourself that kind of happiness."

"Maybe." It comes out all strangled and breathless because I'm still crying—and for what? For a love I can't have even though it's right there within my grasp?

CHAPTER 26
Jamie

I bake and I bake. I knead batch after batch of dough, until I can't feel my arms anymore, and a persistent layer of flour is crusted under my fingernails. Making sourdough is a slow process and it allows me a lot of time to mull things over. Did I really bail on Mac again? In a way, I did, but what was I supposed to do? Should I have been more patient? I could have been. But I'm not the type to take things lying down like that—not even for Mac. I'm a woman of action. Someone who likes to take charge of things. Waiting for Mac to trample all over my heart with all her doubts and trepidations is not my style.

Perhaps I was also foolish enough, for a while there, to believe she might change her mind about me. Although, deep down, I knew she wouldn't. I felt it even when we were in bed together, after those rare moments when she was able to let go of the past, and just be with me and enjoy what we had. Afterward, Mac always pulled away. She always raised her guard all the way up again and it hurt me more every single time.

I try to keep Sandra's perspective in mind, however. It's the only thing that keeps me from not overworking this dough until it's no longer good for anything. Should I fight for Mac? And is the fact that I even have to ask myself that question not an answer in itself? But it's okay that I'm not totally sold on the idea. I don't have to be. It doesn't have to be black-and-white like that—I don't have to be so like Mac about it. I left her twenty years ago so I'm surely going to do that again—or odds are that I will. It's such utter bullshit.

There's just as much chance Mac would leave me, for whatever reason. That's how life is. So many marriages end in divorce, for all kinds of reasons. All those couples who made vows to each other, and for what? I understand her fear but I don't know how to address it. I can't make her love me in the way that she needs in order to give us another chance. Because how do you prove that you can be trusted? It's not possible and that's the crux of her issue with me—with us.

What I can do, is make her a loaf of the best bread she's ever had. I'll even make it in the shape of a heart. Write a message on it. Just so she knows I'm thinking of her—and that I do love her.

The first text I get from Mac reads:

I loaf you? Really?

It's quickly followed by another.

> I'm still chuckling, by the way. I also really don't want to cut into this bread. It's too gorgeous.

I reply:

> I can bring you another, less romantic one.
> 😃

I stop myself from adding: *Right now, if you want to.*

It takes a while before she replies to my last message. It just says:

> Thank you.

At least we're in touch again. That's something. Neither one of us might know any more than we did when we said goodbye almost a week ago, but it's better to be in contact with her than not, that much I do know. To have this tiny line of communication open between us, even if it doesn't lead to anything else than exchanging a text message from time to time. Although I did say that I love her—well, *loaf her*. Surely, she knows what it means. Surely, she knows how I feel.

I'm about to bring a loaf upstairs to Miss Carol when my phone rings. I nearly drop the bread I'm carrying, because who knows? It might be *her*.

I fumble for my phone in my pocket. It *is* her. As soon as I pick up, Mac starts talking.

"I don't want to see you, Jamie, for obvious reasons, but maybe we can talk. Over the phone."

"Not even on FaceTime?" I might as well skip the greeting as well.

"No. You're…" She sighs heavily. "Well, you're basically too hot."

"Of all the things a person can be accused of." I put the bread away and settle in the couch.

"I don't trust myself around you." Mac chuckles. "It's not all *your* fault. I have this inexplicable weakness when it comes to you. I've been thinking about seeing a doctor but I'm too embarrassed to explain my problem, namely that I keep ending up in bed with my ex."

Has she been drinking? Her words come through perfectly clear, not a hint of slurring about them. I decide to play along—because this is so much more fun than nursing my broken heart. Maybe, depending on how this call goes, it doesn't have to remain so broken.

"I sure hope you don't have to call in sick to work," I say. "I'd hate missing your pretty face on TV." This isn't just bantering that we're doing. It's full-on flirting.

"I'll be out of town to cover the Athletics Championships next week. I'll be all over your screen, if you want to see me."

"Oh, I do want to see you."

"It's in Seattle so there's not much chance of running into you, which will be good for my curious affliction."

"We should start a support group, because I seem to be suffering from the exact same disorder."

"Nothing but impure thoughts when you see Jamie Sullivan?" Mac bursts out laughing. "I imagine it's a lot harder for you to deal with, unless you get rid of all the mirrors in your place."

I chuckle along because it feels so good. "My condition is much worse than yours, actually. All I have to do is switch on my TV and there you are."

"You don't *have* to switch on your TV."

"Yeah right."

A short silence falls. Maybe Mac has run out of steam. It's hard to gauge when I can't see her face—that face I know so well.

"Both Leila and Alan have been laying into me," she says after a while. "Basically telling me that I'm a fool." She does an intake of breath and I'm not sure if it's a chuckle or something else. "You won't believe what Leila said to me."

"I'm all ears." My pulse quickens.

"She said that instead of just my legs, I should also open my heart to you."

I burst out laughing. I should send Leila a really nice loaf of bread for saying that. "No, she didn't," I say.

"She fucking did." Mac laughs along. She must think it's funny, otherwise she wouldn't have shared it with me, of all people. "Can you believe that?"

Can I ask Mac what her reply was? Or will that instantly kill the pleasant vibe of this phone call? I'm too curious. "Leila's quite something. What was your response to this outrageous statement?"

"That I stopped opening my legs to you," Mac deadpans and it's hilarious and sad at the same time.

A tense hum is all I can manage, because even though we're just talking on the phone, I can feel the potential of us, what Mac and I could be together, vibrate on this invisible line between us.

"She said I was a fool. So did Alan, although he used other words."

What am I supposed to say to that? I stay silent because I have no say in this—and I said my piece to Mac the last time I saw her.

"How are you feeling?" I ask, instead.

"I've never been so happy with a loaf of bread," Mac says.

"Good." The conversation is losing steam. Probably because we're about to reach the same dead end again.

"Is it okay that I called you?" Mac asks.

"It's very okay."

"Can I call you when I'm in Seattle?"

"I'll look forward to it."

"Maybe we can FaceTime, because I'll be a safe two and a half thousand miles away?"

"Sure. Let's treat it as an experiment to see what happens when we communicate via screen."

"See if it compels us to tear off our clothes and have FaceTime sex," Mac says.

I'd very much like to go over to Mac's apartment right now and tear off all my—and her—clothes.

"Sorry," Mac says when I don't immediately respond —she doesn't know what I'm thinking. "Did I go too far?"

"No, um, it's a date. I mean, not an actual date, of course."

"A FaceTime date. A fully clothed FaceTime date."

"I look forward to it."

"Me too," Mac says, and then we hang up.

Instead of analyzing what that call meant, I think it better to distract myself and make another loaf of bread.

CHAPTER 27
Mac

J amie and I have been texting back and forth since I called her a couple of days ago. I've just arrived at my hotel in Seattle and I should prepare for a long day tomorrow, but all I can think of is FaceTiming her. As the days have gone by, I've started suffering from a brand-new affliction: elaborately fantasizing about Jamie Sullivan every moment of the day.

When she sent me the I-loaf-you bread, I simply had to respond. Things spiraled into this from there. I'm feeling a little unhinged, definitely frisky, but most of all, I can't wait to hear her voice—and see her face, albeit on a tiny screen.

Even though that's very unfair to Jamie, I'm not sure what my end game is. She put her cards on the table and I know what she wants: me. I can blame it on that loaf all I want—at her instigating contact when I wasn't expecting it—but that would be very hypocritical. I'm not immune to what my friends tell me. I'm most certainly not immune to Jamie.

I take a quick shower, and I'm of half a mind to just

slip on the hotel robe for our call—that's how giddy I am —but that would definitely be out of line. I put on regular clothes, grab my phone, and tap the FaceTime icon.

"Hey." For a moment, all I see are Jamie's bangs and her gorgeous bedroom eyes. "There you are," she says.

"And you." Sometimes, like earlier on the plane when Jamie occupied all my thoughts, I think Leila might be right. That I'm a fool to squander a love like this. "How are you?"

"I'm okay." Jamie sounds more serious than she did on our last call. Maybe because we can see each other—or maybe because I didn't give her much choice last time. "You?"

"Happy to see your face." My heart's pitter-pattering inside my chest and my palms are so clammy, I can barely hold on to my phone. I miss her, which I can admit to myself, but not to her. "Are you sure I wasn't too forward on our last call?"

"I'm just going with the flow here, Mac. I have no expectations and I trust you will respect the boundaries I've set."

You might have to reset those, I think, but definitely do not say out loud.

"Let me rephrase," I say. "Part of me knows very well I was too forward, but it was just so good to talk to you. So much fun."

"Can I ask you something?" Jamie runs a hand through her lustrous hair.

"Shoot." I nestle into the pillows and try to relax.

"My upstairs neighbor, Miss Carol, who is also my landlady and friend—"

"Miss Carol of the delicious home-cooked meals delivered to your door?"

"Yes, her. What would you say if, um, I told you she wants to invite me to dinner so I can meet a friend of her daughter's that she thinks I would hit it off with?"

What's happening? Did this call beam me into a different dimension? I was secretly hoping for FaceTime sex, not Jamie telling me her landlady wants to arrange a blind date for her.

"What would I say to that?" Is this some sort of test? "Is this a purely hypothetical situation?" My heart hammers furiously against my ribcage for very different reasons now. If it was Jamie's intention to make me jealous, she has succeeded.

"No," Jamie says drily. "She asked me last night."

"What did you say?"

"That I had to think about it."

I'm trying to keep my cool, even though I have no right to be even a little angry about this. When I got asked out on a date the other week, at least I had the decency to say no immediately, because of Jamie. Clearly, she doesn't want to extend me the same courtesy. And why should she?

"Have you thought about it?" I ask.

"I don't have to think about it, Mac. I was just letting her down easy, but it's an interesting situation, don't you think?"

My muscles relax, but only a fraction. "What are you really asking me?"

"I'm asking how you would feel if I went on a date with someone else." She's done mincing her words, then. I thought that, at least for the time I was away, we could keep this light and fun—possibly even sexy. But I'm not the only one in this *interesting* situation.

"I would be quite upset."

"Even though you don't want to be with me?"

I wish we weren't on FaceTime. I feel like she's calling my bluff and my poker face is crumbling quickly.

"Jamie, what are you doing?" I square my shoulders.

"I'm telling you about something that happened in my life."

I shake my head. I can't say that's not something I want to hear, even though it's decidedly not.

"I assumed that maybe you wanted to be friends," Jamie continues. "Since you called me the other day."

"I called you because you sent me a loaf of bread that said that you loved me." It sounds ridiculous to say out loud, yet that's what Jamie did—and I love her for it.

"This is not a trick or an ambush or anything like that. I'm only telling you I got asked out, just like you did last week."

"After which you promptly decided you no longer wanted to see me." What are we doing? How come we always end up back here, running circles around each other?

"You know why."

"And you know why we can't be together."

"Then maybe you should learn not to be jealous when I do go out with someone else," Jamie says. Her words cut me like the sharpest knife.

"I'm always going to be jealous," I blurt out. "If I'm not over you by now, I'm never going to get over you."

"I'm all out of arguments, Mac. And I'm getting tired of this not-so-merry-go-around." Jamie sinks her front teeth into her lip and for the first time ever, it doesn't make me want to kiss her. Not only because I physically can't, but also because she's right—and it hurts like hell.

"I loaf you too," I say, because I'm all out of arguments as well and it's all I can think of. But it's not funny under these circumstances.

"Then take the leap. Stop making yourself—and me—so miserable with all this dwelling in the past." Jamie attempts a tight smile before continuing. She looks vulnerable and a little wounded. "I'm not asking you to marry me, Mac. All I'm asking is that you give me a chance. That you try to get past all that's holding you back. For us. Please."

I can't say no to Jamie any longer. I've worn myself down with my boundless desire for her and that ugly pang of jealousy I just experienced. If I have to choose between the two—and Leila's right about this, at least—I'd be a fool to choose the latter. I want to choose love and joy, for once in my life after our break-up.

Don't look too far ahead, I tell myself. Look at Jamie's face on the screen. And say yes already.

"I'll try," I say.

Jamie's big eyes go wider still, as though she has seen the most badass ghost. "You will?" She leans closer to the camera. "Mac? You will?" Her voice breaks.

"I can't make you any promises, but I will try. I want to."

"Oh my god." Jamie heaves a huge sigh. "Why aren't you here right now?"

All I can give her in return is a smirk.

"Should I hop on a plane?" Jamie asks. "That affliction we talked about last time has suddenly gotten so much worse. I might not live if I don't kiss you within the next twenty-four hours."

"We've waited twenty years." I sink back into the pillows. A huge weight has been lifted off my shoulders—

205

a weight I kept in place for far too long. "What's another week?"

"That'll give me a chance to polish The Thing," Jamie says. The fragile look in her eyes from earlier has transformed into a naughty spark.

"For an entire week?" I ask in between giggles.

"What else am I going to do with myself?" Her face becomes serious again. "You have an entire week to change your mind."

"I'm sick of changing my mind." Admittedly, my track record in this department hasn't been stellar since I've seen Jamie again. "I want to be with you, Jamie." Even though I'm terrified, I think. Even though I'm filled to the brim with doubts. But my desire for Jamie is far bigger.

"Maybe it's good that you have a week to think it over," Jamie says.

"For you as well," I say.

"No." Jamie shakes her head. "I know exactly what I want. No one compares to you, Mac. I want you."

"I want you too," I say and, for the first time, it feels right.

CHAPTER 28
Jamie

Who knew seven days could feel like seven lifetimes? Mac and I spoke on the phone every day, but she wasn't in Seattle for a holiday and I'm quickly learning how full-on her job is. Mac's not just a pretty face on TV telling viewers what happened in the world of sports. She knows her stuff. She's a master at it. And she works damn hard. Maybe that's why she bought that glitzy apartment that, in my opinion, doesn't suit her one bit. Her priorities in life have certainly shifted. The Mac I knew didn't care about a fancy place to live. She cared about me, our future, and her job. In that order.

As I pace through my living room, waiting for time to pass, my mind wanders to when she came to my hotel room. When she stated she didn't care about me or my feelings any longer. It sounded so plausible when she said it, but it didn't take long for her to start contradicting herself. She's been doing that ever since. So, of course I'm scared she'll change her mind. But I also know I'm nowhere near as frightened as she is. So many outcomes are possible. And love doesn't exist without risk.

Finally, my phone beeps with a message telling me Mac's plane has landed. Depending on traffic, she'll be home in an hour—and she has the next four days off. My heart skips another beat.

I grab my bag, and the groceries I bought, and start walking. I'll arrive at her building well before she does, but I couldn't stay at home any longer. I can't wait to feel her skin against my hands. Her lips against mine. Most of all, I can't wait to wake up next to her tomorrow and know that when I look at her, when I see her lying next to me, that's where she wants to be—and wants to stay.

She wants to try. We're both going to try, but the leap is bigger for Mac. It holds more risk even though I'd rather never bake another loaf in my life than hurt Mac again. Although I can't predict the future, I know, in my heart of hearts that I will never cheat on her again. Certain life lessons are so painful, a repeat offense is simply not an option.

Perhaps it was a touch cruel of me to tell Mac about Miss Carol and her proposition, but Sandra urged me to fight for her—and that's what I was doing. It wouldn't be the first time Miss Carol tried to set me up with someone, despite me repeating that I'm very happily single. At least, I was until I saw Mac again. Miss Carol knows me well, which is why she insisted more than usual.

"If that fancy lady off the TV doesn't want to be with you, I'll find you someone who'd be delighted to," she said. "In fact, I know just the person."

Things snowballed from there, and I might have ended up having dinner at Miss Carol's one night, but I would never have said yes to an actual date with someone else. Not when my mind is so full of all things Mac. Even though, perhaps, it shouldn't be. But something happened when I saw her again. That very first split second when I laid eyes on her again after twenty years. I was trying so hard to keep my cool around her, to give her a hug with just the right amount of strength. But in my head, I was already falling apart.

Because it's always been her. Despite my other relationships, and the life I've lived since screwing things up with her. Despite learning to live with the fact that Mac would hate me forever. That I hurt the woman I loved more than anything so callously, so profoundly, that she never wanted to see me again.

Odd as it may sound, Mac and I had a clean, swift break the first time. She simply refused to see me again. She was too shell-shocked. Too stunned by what I had done. Our friends put up a shield around her and made it so Mac didn't even have to talk to me. My father collected my belongings from the apartment Mac and I had shared for years. I will always remember him saying there was no work left for him to do when he arrived at our place. Mac had already packed up all my stuff. Every last little item, including all the things we'd bought together—so she wouldn't have anything to remember me by.

I can't blame Mac for wanting to pretend I never existed, even though we spent ten amazing years together. I took away the things that mattered to her. At the time, most of our friends naturally sided with her, and she had a job she loved, but she lost everything else when I left. When I burned down all our plans for the future.

As I approach Mac's building, I'm hit with the memory of her face on that fateful day. How it went from disbelief to denial to glacial stoicism. How, in a matter of seconds, she built a wall around her heart, so that I could never get through—and hurt her—again.

As I stand in front of Mac's building, I realize that I don't deserve this. I don't deserve her. For her to let me back in, after I did the worst to her, makes her even more beautiful. Too beautiful for the likes of me. Yet, here I am. A chill runs along my spine, reminding me of how physical this whole thing has been. How, perhaps, our bodies have brought us back together before our minds could. But once we're past this initial lust, this needing each other to the extent that we can't wait to forget the past, we will have a lot to deal with. What I did to Mac is not something that can be swept under the rug. It's not something we can ignore and live happily ever after with. Not for her, but also not for me.

I went through other breakups after Mac, but they were very different. Time always brought relief and a new sense of calm, whereas the years after Mac, long after Cherry and I had split, only brought regret. In my head, I fabricated grand plans to win Mac back, but as soon as I tried anything, be it sending a text message, or even just asking a mutual friend about her, I got shut down. Someone always told me off and put me in my place by reminding me what I had done. If not my own father, then Sandra, or Alan even, or someone else who'd seen Mac through the worst. All the people who were on my case when I chose Cherry. No one was on my side—only Cherry.

Because it was always so easy to see what Mac and I had. As though the strength of our relationship carried over onto our friends and family, as though the wholesomeness of our life made the lives of the people around us better through some magical transference. And, along with Mac, everyone else was shocked into detesting me as well.

It didn't help that I failed to rationally explain to anyone, including myself, why I chose Cherry, whom I barely knew, over Mac, my future wife. When I did it, when I made the worst choice of my life, the reason was crystal clear to me, though. Falling madly in love with Cherry might not have been a good enough reason for anyone else, but it was for me.

Because my love for Mac had always been so present and pure, I didn't know how else to deal with another woman encroaching on that. I didn't know there was another option to deal with it. I didn't know that falling in love with another person can happen when you're already in a relationship. I didn't know that it didn't have to be the end of everything. How could I possibly get into bed with Mac when all I could think of was Cherry? How could I even look her in the eye again after Cherry and I had slept together? I might have been able to if being with Cherry hadn't felt like I was being catapulted into the sky to spend some time among the stars. If she hadn't shown me, made it vibrate in every cell of my body, that it wasn't only Mac who could make me feel like that. At least I believed so at the time.

All my mistakes run through my head, but I let them. I've had twenty years to come to terms with what I did, and I may have needed every single day of them, but I'm ready to put the past behind me. I'm ready to find out if what we had can be reinvented as the people we are now.

Because I want Mac. We have so much unfinished business. And she's finally willing to give me another chance. There's no way I'm letting the past catch up with me. I'm ready for the future.

CHAPTER 29
Mac

I nearly trip over my feet stumbling out of the cab. I can't waste one more second before I fall into Jamie's arms. I might have had a week to change my mind, but I've done the opposite. By saying those words I thought I'd never say to her, by agreeing to try, I flipped a switch inside me. Instead of increasing, my doubts have shrunk. Because I can't forget her and, this time around, I don't have to. This time around, she's choosing me. This time around, there's no Cherry to take her away from me. Jamie is here, for me, in all her glory. She's right there, chatting to the doorman, waiting for me.

Jamie grins from ear to ear when I bolt toward her. Neither one of us has changed her mind. Maybe this is the most foolish I've ever been in my life, but I don't care, because it feels right.

When I fall into Jamie's arms, it feels exactly as it should. Unquestionably, unequivocally right. I want to hurry upstairs so I can kiss her, tear those clothes from her and drag her into the shower with me, but it's not the prevailing urge coursing through me. My physical desire for her is cut through with another kind of longing. I want to get to know her all over again. Now that my mind is finally giving me a chance to look beyond the ruins of our past, I have a million questions. All the questions I didn't allow myself to ask because I didn't want to get too attached. I made myself believe what we had between us was more physical than anything else, even though it clearly wasn't. But I can forgive myself for my ignorance. Fear breeds shortsightedness and I simply couldn't see. But standing in Jamie's arms like this, out here on the sidewalk, I see and I know.

I know what I have to do. What Leila told me: open my heart to Jamie. To gorgeous, kind, sexy Jamie. I'd be a fool not to, because a love like this only comes along once in a lifetime—because there's only one Jamie Sullivan.

"It's so good to see you," Jamie whispers in my ear. Her arms are locked around me, as though she doesn't plan on letting go of me anytime soon.

"The elevator's waiting for you, Miss Mackenzie," the doorman says. "Your suitcase's inside."

"We should probably get out of the street." I wriggle myself out of Jamie's embrace. "Come on." I take her hand and drag her into the elevator. As soon as the doors close, she comes for me again. My lips are stretched into a persistent grin, making it hard to kiss her—if ever there was a first-world problem.

Hand in hand, we ride the elevator. To be so free of doubts is a revelation, like a new light is being shed on everything. Jamie looks so much better in real life than on my tiny phone screen. Her touch is intoxicating. Her hair shinier. Her eyes dreamier.

We hurry into my apartment, abandoning our bags in the hallway.

"I have to shower," I protest, but only meekly.

"We'll shower together later," Jamie says, "after this." We don't even make it into the bedroom. She pushes me against a wall and, with the corner of a picture frame pressing into my arm, she kisses me again. It's a kiss full of pent-up lust, not just a week's worth, but two decades' worth. Because I finally said yes, and my yes shines through in this kiss. In how we touch each other, in our hunger for each other, and the intention behind it.

I hold Jamie close, luxuriating in the warmth of her body, the softness of her skin. Our kiss doesn't stop. Her tongue keeps darting in and out of my mouth, her lips keep finding mine. Her hand starts to wander down, and she opens the button of my jeans.

Jamie groans into my mouth as her fingers slide inside my panties. She sounds as turned on as I feel. Maybe I should check for myself. I return the favor and unzip her pants. When I slip my hand inside, our kiss stalls. Jamie takes a moment to breathe, to look at me. Our eyes lock and it's more intimate than any kiss. It's hotter than her lips trailing along the sensitive skin of my neck.

We peer into each other's eyes as our hands explore further. As our fingers dive deeper. As we mirror each other's actions. My finger edges along Jamie's clit, before sliding deeper into her wetness.

She does the same to me.

All the while, I can see the expression on her face. That dark sparkle lighting up her eyes. The fullness of her lips. That barely-there freckle on the side of her mouth. The ferocity with which she wants me. What it has done to her for me to say yes, that I will try. We've taken the next step. Because I don't want to lose her. I want her in my life. Despite the fear that resides in my flesh, lurks under my skin. If the past few weeks have taught me anything it's that what I believed was a choice, isn't a matter of choosing at all.

Jamie slips a finger inside me, and I have to catch my breath. But I keep looking at her. The shape of her mouth changes with the effort she's exerting. Two can play at that game, I think, and push a finger high inside her.

"Oh, fuck," she says on a sigh. She puts her other hand on my shoulder, holding onto it, as though she needs the support—as though she's already getting there.

Her finger slips out of me and circles my clit. She wants me right there with her. All I have to do is look at her face and surrender to her touch. Two things I never thought I'd do again, and look at me now. The unpredictability of life isn't just shocking. It can be astounding as well. And hot. Jamie is so hot with her face contorted like that, with her desire on full display.

Does she feel as vulnerable as I do with the walls around my heart quickly crumbling? I'm letting my guard down all the way. I'm letting go of the last ounce of protection against her, and all my senses are on high alert. Every small movement she makes feels big, overwhelming, and inevitable. A bit like this situation was inevitable. Like us, standing against this wall, unable to keep our hands to ourselves, so close despite years of hostility.

All I can do is let the last twenty years collapse in on themselves. Let all the tension in my muscles dissolve and give myself to her. Because Jamie's doing exactly the same. She digs her fingertips deep into the flesh of my shoulder as she holds on, as she rides this swift but strong—and equally inevitable—climax with me.

"Hello to you, too," Jamie says as she buttons up her jeans.

I shake my head while I try to straighten my clothes. Normally, after a week of non-stop work away from home, I take a few days to myself to recharge, but this time around, Jamie's here.

"Remember Maui?" I say.

"I will never, ever forget Maui."

I chuckle. "When I said you must have magic voodoo fingers?" I reach for her hand.

"Every single thing you said is etched into my memory." Jamie always liked a touch of exaggeration to make a point.

I take her hand and study her long, strong fingers. A frisson of something runs up my spine again. Now that I'm letting myself feel everything, my body is like a live wire, the smallest touch causing a spark.

"Turns out I was right," I say.

"Your fingers aren't too bad either." Jamie smiles at me with her entire face. Her eyes seem to catch all the light streaming through the windows and she beams it right back at me.

I'm so in love with her. It's happening all over again. All the reasons I loved her are still there. I feel like a teenager in love for the first time. All I can do at the sight of her, at the soft sensation of her hand in mine, is utter a silly giggle.

"What's going on with you?" Jamie asks, unable to suppress a smile—because she knows full well what's going on.

"I'm going to take a long shower. Probably a cold one."

"If it's going to be cold, I'm not joining you." She

grins at me. "I will thoroughly wash my hands and prepare you a meal. How does that sound?"

"As long as you don't ask me where anything is in the kitchen," I joke.

"I wouldn't dare." She raises our joined hands and kisses the inside of my wrist.

"Make yourself at home," I say. My apartment looks so different—so much more like a home—with Jamie in it.

"I will. Thank you." Every word she says, makes me fall deeper in love with her. "I love you," Jamie says, just like that.

CHAPTER 30
Jamie

I've made us a simple stir-fry of shrimp and vegetables with whatever condiments I could find in Mac's swanky kitchen. Fresh sourdough I brought from home on the side. I may not be too crazy about the overall vibe of her apartment, but the kitchen is top-notch —and entirely wasted on someone like Mac who never cooks.

"Sandra said I had to fight for you." To sit across from her, just the two of us, sharing a meal, feels as intimate as what we did out in the hallway earlier. "According to her, I was bailing on you again."

"Poor San," Mac says. "I don't know how she has managed all these years, being a friend to us both."

"I assume you and she didn't discuss me all that much?" It's impossible to look away from Mac. Her hair's still wet from the shower and slicked back, kind of like her hairdo at Sandra's wedding, when she looked to die for.

"No, although that wasn't always my choice. When I finally did start asking about you, Sandra made it very clear that she wasn't going to do that with me. For the sake of our friendship, you were off limits in conversation," Mac says.

"Same here. Well, after a while, at least." The earfuls Sandra gave me after I chose Cherry left almost as big a scar as my break-up from Mac. "It wasn't easy for her."

"Why do you think she finally relented?" Mac asks.

"She didn't relent. Enough time had passed for her to ask both of us to be there on her big day. For once, she was only thinking about herself, and good for her."

"Yeah." Mac looks at her fork full of food. "This is delicious, by the way. Has anyone ever said you should do something in food?"

"There was this blonde back in the day," I play along. "Hot as hell. A body like you wouldn't believe. She had some sway over me, and I let her talk me into pursuing my dream of becoming a baker."

"Because of her hot body?" Mac pretends to be outraged.

I nod. "She was a college athlete, so I was pretty much defenseless against all those delicious muscles."

"Hm." Mac puts down her fork. "Can you tell me some more about this person? Would I have known her?"

"Oh, yeah." I gaze into Mac's eyes. I can still so easily see the woman I fell in love with back then. "You wouldn't have been able to resist her either."

Mac chuckles and puts down her fork. She reaches out her hand. "Just to be clear, I don't think you bailed on me again."

I take her hand in mine and it reminds me of how we used to be. Always touching. Always in contact. Her skin against mine is instantly soothing.

"I understand why Sandra would put it that way,

though." I hold onto Mac's hand a little tighter. "But I'm not going to bail on you anytime soon. Not if I can help it."

Mac just nods. Maybe she doesn't believe me, or maybe she just needs more time before she can. "There was not much to bail on, was there?" She traces a finger-nail over the inside of my hand. "I was doing what I've always done since we broke up." She exhales dramatically. "I never thought it would feel so good to just let it all go." She pauses. "And maybe, paradoxically, I can only let it all go with you."

"If only Sandra had gotten married ten years earlier," I say.

A shadow crosses Mac's face. "Life goes the way it goes."

"You're right. We should be happy Sandra and Tyrone finally tied the knot. It took them long enough to find each other."

"I was absolutely terrified when I arrived in Maui," Mac says. "I didn't want to leave the airport. For a brief moment, I considered taking the first flight back." She traps one of my fingers between hers. "I was so afraid of what seeing you again would do to me. As though, subconsciously, I already knew it would totally undo me. Although I would never have been able to admit that to anyone, especially myself."

"It's been quite the ride since, but here we are." I go all mellow inside.

"I wish I could promise you a smoother ride from here on out, but that's not a promise I can make right now." Mac exhales slowly. "Although I can hardly claim that I want to go slowly."

"It will take the time it takes for you to be able to trust

me fully again, Mac, but we have time." We have the rest of our lives.

"Please tell your landlady you're taken now." Mac paints on a smirk.

"Oh, she knows." I might have bounded up the stairs and knocked on Miss Carol's door like I'd just won the lottery after that FaceTime call with Mac. "You're kind of cute when you're jealous, by the way."

"You're just saying that because of the outcome of this particular bout of jealousy." Mac swallows slowly. "I've wasted a lot of my life on jealous, paranoid nonsense."

"It's not nonsense. As you just said, life goes the way it goes and…" I hold on tightly to her hand, hoping it's better than another apology. "Who knows? Maybe Alan was right. If you and Leila had stayed together, she wouldn't have saved Isabel Adler."

Mac narrows her eyes. "Leila is a very attractive woman." She shakes her head. "We could have been good together under different circumstances." She pulls her lips into a devilish smirk.

"Are you trying to make *me* jealous?" I ask.

Mac shrugs. "Is it working?"

"I'm jealous of everyone who got to be with you. Hell, I was jealous of your co-hosts on TV, because they got to spend time with you and I didn't."

"I've always been so focused on my own pain." Mac's voice has lowered. "I was so angry with you for such a long time, I never stopped to consider yours."

"The difference is that I'm the one who caused it." I can look Mac in the eye and say that now.

"Still, it must have hurt like hell." She takes my hand fully in hers, enveloping it, as though she wants to keep it safe from something.

"It did." This moment is so beautiful, with my hand wrapped in Mac's, and the both of us being able to acknowledge our hurt, it repairs something inside of me.

"I made a lot of mistakes too." She slants her head, then cradles my hand tighter in hers. "God, Jamie, I should have forgiven you years ago. I should have taken you back after your thing with Cherry ended. I should have—"

"Mac," I interrupt her. "You couldn't. I know this because you would have if you'd been able to, but, ironically, I think, because of the depth of our love, because of how incredibly good we were together, you couldn't just do that."

Her eyes are moist.

"Besides," I continue, "it doesn't matter anymore now. Those years have gone by. Time has been relentless. Speaking of…" It's probably a good idea to lighten the mood a bit. "Your big Five Oh is just around the corner."

Mac huffs out some air. "I didn't really mind that I'm about to turn fifty, because I've done a lot of the things I wanted to do in my life, but…" The sadness that lurks in her voice might very well be one I can never relieve. "I mean, realistically, forty was already kind of a cut-off date, but there were still options. Now that I'm on the cusp of fifty, it's definitive. Not that I even want to become a mother now, but it's quite the harsh reminder of what I wanted and the one thing I didn't do with my life."

So much for lightening the mood. Maybe bringing up Mac's upcoming fiftieth wasn't the best of moves, considering. But there has to be room for regret—no one lives a life without it.

A silence falls and we both let it envelop us. I, too,

think about all the things I didn't have, but also about all the things I do.

"You know what I want for my birthday?" Mac says after a while.

"An I-loaf-you loaf?" I joke.

"Aside from that, obviously, and perhaps also some of your infamous carrot cake." A smile has reappeared on her face, like the sun breaking through the clouds after days of drizzle. "I want to go away with you. Just the two of us. Do you think that place on Rockaway Beach still exists?"

Is she referring to the spot where I asked her to marry me?

"I can look it up right now." My tone is hesitant. Do we really want to revisit that specific memory?

"It's probably nothing like how I remember it," Mac says. "But I'd like to see for myself."

"Whatever you want, babe." I put my free hand on hers. "It's your birthday."

"Before that, however, I think I should take you home. To my mother."

"Oh, damn." I may smile, but Suzanne was always a formidable force. I never spoke to her again, but it was easy enough to imagine how she felt about me after what I did. "I'm not sure I'm ready to charm Suzanne."

"You'll never be ready, but it's best to get it over with." Is Mac delighting in this?

"Okay. I'll face Suzanne. Bring it on."

"I've been working on her," Mac says. "Smoothing the path for the moment you see each other again."

"That's a relief," I lie.

"Her bark's always been worse than her bite." Mac is definitely having fun with this.

"Please, stop," I say, although facing Mac's mother is a small price to pay for being back in her life—for the chance to be with her again and not fuck up this time.

CHAPTER 31
Mac

M y mother is neither demure, nor predictable—especially when it comes to her reaction to Jamie. I'm not as nervous as Jamie, who's doing a fairly good job of keeping her cool, but I'm not as relaxed as usual when I go to see my mom. But it's my birthday celebration and my mother always wants to make me feel like a million bucks for the occasion.

I might have been a latchkey kid who learned to prepare a makeshift dinner by the age of twelve—this is why I dislike cooking to this day—but birthdays were always a big deal in our family of two. My mother always made me feel like a princess, no matter how busy she was.

We're sitting in the car outside my mom's house.

Jamie puffs up her cheeks, then lets the air escape slowly. "Okay. Let's do this."

"Hey." I put a hand on her knee. "My mom knows what you mean to me. It'll be all right." I squeeze Jamie's knee. "She just wants me to be happy, and you make me happy." I understand it's daunting for Jamie to see my mother again. It's not like the other night when Jamie's dad called and asked to speak to me, his voice shaky with emotion.

"Thank goodness I'm charming," Jamie jokes, but her heart's not fully in it.

"And you brought half a bakery worth of goodies."

We collect the bags of bread, cake, and biscuits—baking was the only way Jamie could cope—and make our way to the front door. It swings open before we can knock.

"Gabby, sweetheart." My mother holds her arms wide. "There's just no way you're fifty years old. It can't possibly be." She ignores Jamie's presence and throws her arms around me. "I could swear I only had you yesterday." She plants a few kisses on my cheek. "Happy birthday, sweetheart." She holds on to me a while longer, as though she doesn't want to let go.

I clear my throat. "Um, Mom?"

She releases me from her hold, then looks over at Jamie. She gives her a once-over. She shakes her head slightly. "Oh, Jamie," she says. "I never thought I'd see the day." To my surprise, she opens her arms to Jamie as well. "Come here."

Jamie puts the bags down and awkwardly steps into my mother's embrace. It's a far cry from the mother-daughter hug we just shared, but it's a whole lot more than I was expecting her to give.

"It's lovely to see you, Ms. Mackenzie," Jamie mumbles.

My mother scoffs. "Really? You're going to Ms. Mackenzie me? I don't think so. It's always been Suzanne to you." She releases Jamie from her hold.

"Suzanne it is," Jamie says, and with that, the top layer of ice seems to be broken.

My mother and Jamie always got along, but when Jamie dumped me, my mother's claws came out. She witnessed the pain it caused me and her maternal instinct was to lash out at Jamie. She reacted how most mothers do when their child gets brutally hurt. But a lot of time has gone by, and my mother has twenty-five more years of life wisdom on me, including the capacity to forgive.

"So this all happened in Maui," Mom says, looking from me to Jamie and back.

We're sitting on the back porch, each with a glass of champagne in our hands.

"Maybe I should go to Maui sometime," my mother continues. "There must be something in the water there."

"Do you have an old flame to rekindle?" I ask.

She just shrugs. "Not for any rekindling, but just to see what miracle would be in store for me." She draws up her eyebrows. "Because that's what this looks like to me." She focuses her gaze on Jamie. "Nothing short of an enormous miracle."

"I'm with you there, Suzanne," Jamie says.

"When Gabby told me you were back in her life, I was shocked, I can tell you that." She slants her head. "Jamie Sullivan. I never thought I'd allow you into my house again."

"I'm over the moon to be here," Jamie says. Under the table, her foot finds me and she hooks her ankle behind mine.

"I'm not without trepidation," my mother says. "Surely, you understand why, but... Well, it somehow makes sense. Seeing the two of you together, it just somehow does." She rests her gaze on me and sends me a quick smile. "The motherly advice I'd like to give you is to not let the years you didn't have come between you now." She lifts her glass. "You're fifty years old, for crying out loud." There's a sudden tremor in her voice. "Nothing I have done in my life compares to you, darling. Nothing. It doesn't even come close." She turns to Jamie. "And you better take care of her. Even though it's the most futile promise to make, I'm still going to need you to promise me, Jamie."

Jamie brings a hand to her chest. "I promise you, with all that I am, that I will treat Mac like the princess she is."

"Damn right," Mom says, and sips from her glass.

"Guys, come on." I'm not entirely unmoved by this, but it's a bit much. "Let's take it down a notch, shall we?" I roll my eyes at their blatant display of sentimentality. Besides, I can protect my own heart. I'm very good at it— too good, maybe.

"Don't pretend this isn't a huge deal, darling." My mother looks at me. "If no one else is going to say it, I will. Because I'm your mother and it's my job."

"I'm fifty, Mom. I think I can take care of myself now." I appreciate her intention, and I get that this is my mother's way of dealing with this—that she has some posturing to do in front of Jamie—but it's also reminding me too much of what happened. Of all the times I drove home to cry on her shoulder. Of all the things I said to her about my dreams being stolen as well as my heart being broken.

"If you want to be a mother, you will find a way," my mother once said. "And if it doesn't happen, you can, in the fullness of time, be at peace with that, too." Her words have been a great comfort to me over the years. Because I clearly didn't find a way to be a mother—and I blamed Jamie for that for a long time. But I'm sitting here with my own mother and Jamie, time not yet full—I'm only fifty—but strangely at peace nevertheless.

CHAPTER 32

Jamie

"Here's to you." I lift my glass, looking from the ocean into Mac's equally blue eyes. The hotel we stayed at twenty years ago, where I asked Mac to marry me, is now a private house with a high fence around it. Instead, I've splashed out on a beach-side rental where we have privacy and an unobstructed view of the ocean.

Mac only turns fifty once and I've missed all of her past twenty birthdays. I have so much to make up for, although, sooner rather than later, I'm going to have to stop seeing it that way. Just as she has let go of her fear, I need to let go of my guilt.

"And to us!" Mac clinks her glass against mine. "The best birthday present ever."

"Also the most unexpected."

"I've always liked surprises, but this really does take the cake." Mac looks as relaxed as our surroundings. It's been a few weeks since she surprised me by saying she wanted to try again, and they couldn't have been more perfect. Morning after morning of waking up next to her.

Night after night of going to bed with her, catching up on all the love we couldn't make. Curling an arm around her warm body in the middle of the night has been the greatest pleasure of all. To have her there, with me, where she should have been all along.

"I love you, Jamie," Mac says.

"And I love you." Simply saying the words doesn't seem adequate enough to express how much I do. I remember feeling exactly the same way twenty years ago, when we first came to this beach, and I had a ring burning a hole in my pocket. Even though I was sure Mac would say yes to my proposal—we'd hinted at it often enough—I was still nervous. The brain can play tricks on you like that. It always tries to find the tiniest 'but'. *I love you, but…*

The times I said that to her when I chose Cherry over Mac—the worst words for any person in love to hear.

It still scares me, too, that despite my love for her, despite asking her to marry me, despite all those undeniable, big feelings I had for her, I left. That I had it in me to hurt us like that. But isn't the biggest triumph of life—and love—that we're sitting here now? I don't have a ring in my pocket but—who knows?—maybe someday I will again.

"It's hard not to think about last time we were here." Mac fixes her gaze on me.

I nod. "I was quite surprised you wanted to come here for your birthday, out of all the places in the world we could have gone."

"Maybe we should have gone back to Maui." Mac chuckles. "All jokes aside, coming to Rockaway is kind of a full circle moment for me. We met Cherry…" I flinch at the mention of her name, but I don't let it show. "Three, four days later?"

And then it all turned to shit. "Hm," I mumble, wondering where she's going with this.

"Then everything changed, even though we didn't really know it yet. But when we were here, when we got engaged, that was probably the last time we fully chose to be with each other." Mac sips from her champagne and it's so at odds with what she's saying—unless I'm being too uptight to miss her point. "That's why I wanted to come here. It might be silly, but returning to that point in time feels like pushing the reset button to before we met her."

"Okay." Mac's neither foolish, nor naive, and I'm far from convinced she actually believes this is possible, but sometimes, the foolish, naive action is the only one you can take.

She must have heard the trepidation in my voice, because she puts her glass down and leans into me. "I promise I'm not punishing you. I'm not interested in that. I'm just trying to find as many ways as possible to come to terms with what happened." She rests her palms on my knees and presses down. "I know I can't turn back the clock and we can't just pick up where we left off, but… it's my birthday week, and I'm indulging myself." She digs her fingertips into the flesh above my knees. "In fact, I'd like to indulge a little more."

I slant toward her, expecting a passionate kiss, but that's not the kind of indulging Mac has in mind.

"Just for a few minutes," Mac says, "I would like to go back in time and revisit the plans we made when we got engaged."

"Are you sure?" I put my hands over hers.

"I am." She looks deep into my eyes.

"Let's do it, then," I say, even though I'm not entirely sure what it is she wants to do.

"I wanted four children, although I would have been happy with three," Mac says.

"I know."

"My dream was a house full of kids with obnoxious names like President and Princess."

I shake my head. "There's no way our kids would have had names like that."

"We'll never know," Mac says.

"True." But still.

"After you left, I held on to that idea of our perfect imaginary family for too long," she says. "I wanted my life to go a certain way and when it didn't, I couldn't pivot. I could have had a President and a Princess, but I can see now that the kids I didn't have were all part of this big idea I had for my future. The one I held you responsible for ruining. So I threw myself into work and here I am, twenty years later. With you. Life goes on, no matter what happens and the choices we make."

"Indeed, here we are." I look into her eyes, because I want her to fully grasp what I'm saying. "I'm sorry for——"

"No." Mac shakes her head. "Let me finish. I need to make my point, babe." She sends me a soft smile. "I don't need another apology. What I'm trying to say is that despite my choices or mistakes, all the decisions I made, whatever the reason behind them, have given me a good life. Ask anyone, any person alive, if their life went the way they wanted it to go. That's not what life is. And, yes, I suffered heartache. You hurt me so much, but guess what? That's also part of the experience. It may have taken me a long time, but I got through it. No matter what it cost me, it was worth it. Because, yes, here we are. So many things could have happened if we'd stayed together. We could have met Cherry later. We could have divorced. We could have not been able to have kids. We could have been the happiest couple alive. The point is, we don't know. But we've found each other again. And I might be slow when it comes to certain things, like feelings." She pauses to send me a silly grin. "Like getting over you, and living without you, and knowing, when I saw you again, that all I wanted was to be with you again. But I got there in the end."

"I get now why you wanted to come here." I lean forward until my forehead rests against Mac's.

"No matter what," Mac says. "You're still the one, Jamie. You always were."

Warmth blooms inside me. "So are you," I whisper.

Mac brings her hand to my chin and tilts it toward her. "Remember what I said when you asked me to marry you?"

"Um, yes?" My lips curl into a smile at the memory.

"A thousand times fucking yes," Mac says. "I'm saying it again now. To being with you."

"Music to my ears." We bridge the tiny gap between us, and kiss, with the roar of the waves in the background, and a string of memories—good and bad, like life—in our hearts.

CHAPTER 33

Mac

I kissed Jamie in Maui. I kissed her many times since in Brooklyn, and now I'm kissing her in Rockaway Beach, Queens. I've been all over the place since Maui. I've fallen apart, again and again, but, as humans do, I've stitched myself back together just as many times. I couldn't have done it for anyone else but for her because, as it turns out, the only person who could mend my soul was the one who ripped it to shreds in the first place. If I can't help but love her, to feel this profound comfort and deep satisfaction around her, then I have to be with her. I have to give her a second chance—I have to try. I'd be a fool not to.

It helps that Jamie, in my humble opinion, is the best kisser in the universe. She must be. No one has kissed me how she has. No kiss has turned me on like hers. No kiss has changed the course of my day, my life, my existence like the very first one we shared, in my dorm room at NYU.

In college, Jamie was all tight jeans and leather jackets —and, already, all bangs falling into her eyes. When I met her at a party, I couldn't take my eyes off her, because she was the coolest girl I'd ever seen—and that's saying something when you go to college in New York City.

She was the opposite of me, the wholesome athlete who almost didn't go to the party in her own dorm because we had a big game two full days later. Soccer was always much more important than anything or anyone else, because if it wasn't for my athletic scholarship, I wouldn't have been at New York University. But then I also wouldn't have met Jamie.

My mother was right when she declared this nothing short of a gigantic miracle. Me being here with Jamie. More than thirty years after spotting her at that party, when our eyes met for the very first time and we didn't have a clue what was happening, what it would be the start of, and how it would shape our lives.

Maybe my life didn't go how I wanted it to go, but it went how it was supposed to go. I've learned that it's not so much a matter of getting over things, but a matter of living through them.

Most importantly, I've learned that it's possible for a heart to heal itself. Perhaps the hardest lesson to learn, but also the most necessary. Because there are no guarantees. I will get hurt again, but I will no longer choose retreat as a coping mechanism. Although shying away from romance has given me a lot in my life. I've covered four Olympic Games, countless world championships in any sport you can think of. I'm the country's go-to expert in women's and men's soccer.

On our very first date, Jamie said I had a face for television, and even though she was just flirting, she was more right than she could have known at the time. I've had more dreams come true than I could ever have imagined

—dreams I didn't even know I had. Different dreams than the ones I always clung to, but beautiful, unexpected dreams nonetheless.

I worked hard but loved cautiously. Maybe it's time to turn that around. I'm ready to love Jamie again without caution. To give her my trust. It's the only way this can work. It's the only way for us to, perhaps, someday have that wedding we never had. At least now it would be an actual wedding, not some stop-gap commitment ceremony with no legal value. We would be each other's spouse. I would be Jamie Sullivan's wife. I would be everything I've ever wanted to be—successful in life and love.

"I brought The Thing," Jamie whispers in my ear.

I smile in response, even though it's not what I want right now. I only want to feel her. Her tongue. Her fingers. Her lips all over me. "Maybe tomorrow," I say in between breathy groans.

Jamie replies by kissing me more deeply. By intensifying the grasp of her hands on my body. By undoing my shirt buttons and pushing me onto the bed. We kiss and kiss and manage to get our clothes off while we do. It's not always like this, but sometimes, like today, there's an urgency to our lovemaking, like we do still have all that time to catch up on. But we can't bring back time. All we can do is enjoy the time we have now and, hopefully, the decades left together.

Jamie's body is glued to mine. She stops kissing me for a moment and gazes into my eyes. I look back at her. She's still as hot as the first time I saw her, when I was convinced she was too cool for me. Jamie's beautiful, no matter the mistakes she made. I forgive her for everything because I want to. Because it's all I want—because she's all I ever wanted.

She brings two fingers to my lips and I instinctively open my mouth. Gently, her fingers slip inside and I twirl my tongue around them. I suck her fingers deep into my mouth, as deep as I want them inside me later.

With nothing but tenderness in her glance, Jamie lets her fingers slide out. Her hand travels between my legs. Her fingertips circle my clit. My breath hitches in my throat. Her fingers dip lower. As she pushes inside, I know that this, too, will always heal my soul. This connection between us that I've never found with anyone else.

A perk of being a regular on TV is getting hit on by the most gorgeous, intriguing women. Some of whom I invited into my bed, but none of them could ever make me feel how Jamie did, because I didn't love them the way I loved Jamie. Maybe they crashed into the wall I raised around myself, and my heart. But that no longer matters. The wall is gone.

From the get-go, from that first kiss in Maui, followed by that embarrassingly quick first climax, my body knew what my brain couldn't possibly accept yet. Jamie has always been the one. It's time I focus on what we can still have rather than on what we didn't.

Right now, all my focus is on her magic voodoo fingers inside me. As though her fingers alone possess the power to, in a matter of minutes, take me there. To the place of highest pleasure. Because I still know her, and she still knows me. Because there are things you don't forget, no matter how much time you spend apart.

"I love you," I groan, as Jamie makes me come again, as only she can.

CHAPTER 34
Jamie

ONE YEAR LATER

Izzy accompanies herself on the piano as she sings "A Breathless Place". The words touch me deep inside. Or maybe I'm moved to my very core because of where I'm standing. In the same spot as Sandra and Tyrone stood a year ago. This time, I'm tying the knot. This time, I'm really marrying Gabrielle Mackenzie.

I look out over the small crowd that we've gathered. Our families and a select group of friends. Alan's sniffling as though he's at a funeral instead of a wedding. Charles puts an arm around him. Sandra's head rests on Tyrone's shoulder. Then my gaze is inevitably drawn back to Mac, the woman I'm marrying, against all odds. She looks magnificent in her white tux. Her hair is slicked back exactly the way I like it. Her shoes are bright red.

"As a small nod to our reacquaintance," Mac said when she showed them to me.

I'll never forget how stunning and unattainable she looked in that red dress a year ago, at this same resort.

How she took off her shoes for that impromptu walk on the beach. How she hiked up her red dress so she could sit on the sand with me. How it very slowly, and then all of a sudden quickly, came to be. How Mac and I got back together again because it's where we belong. How we had to get over all our issues, and there were many, but we made it, because, this time, we let love win.

A smile spreads on my lips when I look at her. I'm going to grow old alongside this woman, this beautiful person who lights up my life every single day.

The song ends and we applaud Izzy. I can call Isabel Adler my friend now. She just performed at my wedding. She and Leila have been a joy to get to know the past year.

"It's time for the wedding vows," the officiant says. "Jamie, you're up first." The officiant nods at me. We've rehearsed everything but this. Mac and I have kept our vows secret from each other, until now.

I take her hands, look into her eyes, block out my surroundings, and start.

"My dearest Mac." My throat's closing up already, but I've got this. I take a second to breathe, then start again. "To stand here with you today is at the same time so unlikely and yet so completely meant to be. This contradiction sums up a lot of our lives, together and apart." I insert a short pause. "Marrying you is the biggest honor of my life, because you are…" My eyes are getting moist. "The most amazing woman I've ever met. You are strong, smart, and gorgeous. You are kind, loving, and capable of the kind of forgiveness that I may not deserve, but you've given me regardless.

"It's a cliché for a reason that this is the most beautiful day of my life, but it's a close second to that day when we were here a year ago, for Sandra and Tyrone's wedding, and I saw you again for the first time, and my life changed all over again. Like it did the day we met." I take another shaky breath. "It's easy enough to believe you and I should not be together. That too much has happened. That I hurt you too much." Tempting though it was to ignore that I once broke Mac's heart in a million pieces, it would have been unbearably dishonest, because whether we like it or not, it's a big part of who we are. "But the fact that we are together, that you still want to marry me, is a huge testament to the power of love. To the kind of love we have between us. I promise you, in front of everyone here, that I will always be the faithful, loving wife you deserve." Mac's blinking a tear out of her eye. She squeezes my hands. "I'm so lucky and proud to be able to call you my wife. I'm so thankful that you decided to give me, and us, another chance. I will never take that—or you—for granted ever again. I love you with all my heart."

A short silence falls, only punctuated by sniffling sounds from our loved ones. The officiant gently prods Mac to recite her vows.

She clears her throat. "If you have butterflies in your stomach, invite them into your heart," Mac begins, already blowing my socks off. "That's exactly what I did after I could no longer deny that you, my darling…" Mac looks deep into my eyes. She's so much better at this than I am, and it makes me go weak at the knees. "…are the cause of so many butterflies in here." She brings a hand to her belly. "I've come to love you with my whole heart again. With a passion that can't really be expressed in words, only in kisses, glances, and years of adventure by your side." She's killing me—and doing a stellar job of expressing her passion in words, despite what she just said.

Tears are streaming down my cheeks, but I don't bother wiping them away. These tears, this emotion, is what we're here for. "What I've learned from you, from us, is that to love is to believe, even though to believe is sometimes hard and always a little foolish, but nevertheless, it's required. And I believe in us with everything I have." Mac takes a beat to swallow something out of her throat. "After all this time, you are still my every dream come true, and I can't wait for the reality we finally get to build together." Mac brings our hands together. "Give me your hand," she says, "And I will give you forever."

CHAPTER 35

Mac

"You put my vows to shame," Jamie—my wife—whispers in my ear after the ceremony has ended.

"It's not a competition, babe." I curl my arms around her neck.

"If you say so." Jamie kisses me on the lips. Everyone oohs and aahs. "What you said was so beautiful." Jamie pulls me to her. "Almost as beautiful as you." She leans into my ear again. "You're one hell of a hot bride, Gabrielle Mackenzie."

"Correction, it's Gabrielle Mackenzie-Sullivan now, Jamie Mackenzie-Sullivan."

"What a mouthful." Jamie kisses me on the cheek. "I might just call you Mac, if that's all right with you."

I nod and take a breath. It's done. Jamie and I are married. Hands joined, we walk by our family and friends. I spot a lot of moist cheeks and crumpled-up tissues. But I wasn't going to marry Jamie using standard vows. We're hardly your standard couple.

I asked her to marry me by hiding a ring in the dough she was working on. There was a small risk of Jamie baking it in the oven, ruining her bread—and the ring as well—but sometimes you just have to take the risk.

It was one of the first loaves she made in the brownstone we bought together. She was still finding her way around the kitchen, getting used to new locations for her ingredients. I was lingering around the kitchen, keeping an eye on her every move.

"The air in this house is no good for my dough. I don't know what's wrong with it." She pushed her fingers into the dough, lifted it up, examined it, then let it drop into the bowl again. "It's all over, babe. My career as I know it. Magic voodoo fingers no more." She grinned at me, indicating she knew full well she was being overly dramatic.

"As long as you still have them where it counts." I tried to keep a lid on my nerves, but my heart was hammering against my chest. Jamie was too absorbed by her failing dough to notice.

"You have such a one-track mind, Mac." Jamie's face contorted. "What the hell is this?" Her fingers dug deeper into the dough. "There's something in here. What the—" She extracted the ring out of the dough—and lost the power of speech for an instant. She fiddled with it, removing as much sticky matter as possible. She glanced at me, then back at the ring. By then, I had the widest grin plastered across my face. "Is this what I think it is?" Jamie stammered.

My throat was closing up, so at first, I could only nod.

"You're proposing?" Jamie's voice was so incredulous, even though we'd just bought a house together, tying us to each other in another way.

I nodded some more, the grin wiped off my face. Tears pricked behind my eyes.

"Oh my god, Mac." Jamie fixed her gaze on me. "A

million times fucking yes." She hurried over to me and looked me in the eyes. "Nothing would make me happier than to marry you." She swallowed something out of her throat. "Although you ruined a perfectly good loaf of bread for it." We burst into chuckles and the moment was perfect, because we were laughing and crying at the same time, for all the right reasons.

The party's in full swing and even though we are the guests of honor, Jamie and I have escaped to the beach together.

"Are you also experiencing a weird case of déjà vu?" Jamie asks.

"The best case possible." It's dark, and her features are partly obscured, but I don't have to see her face to know how gorgeous she is. I know every last inch of her face, her body, her smell.

Our engagement was just long enough to accommodate a destination wedding. Version two of our courtship was short—less than a year—but oh-so powerful.

"If I remember correctly, I was quite buzzed on weed the last time." Jamie chuckles.

"You and all your bad habits," I joke.

"Hey." She tugs me toward her. "I don't take any of this lightly. Marrying you is the most important thing I will ever do in my life."

"I know." Turns out trusting Jamie again was easy. She wasn't the problem any longer. Once I got out of my own way, neither was I. When I look at her, I can't even imagine I used to think of her as the woman who stole my dreams, because now, one year later, she has made the biggest one come true. Because she's the person I'm meant to be with. Twenty years apart have surely taught me that. "I love you, Jamie," I say.

"I know what you had to get over to arrive at this place. To marry me today," Jamie continues. "It's the most beautiful thing anyone has ever done for me."

"Nu-huh." I bring my face a mere inch away from hers. "The best is yet to come, babe." Jamie makes it sound as though me forgiving her was for her sake only, but I've also given myself the greatest gift. To no longer have to carry all that insecurity and pain with me, to just let it all go, and win her back in the process, has been the best thing I've ever done for myself.

"I believe you." Jamie touches the tip of her nose against mine. "Do you know why?"

I know what she's going to say—she's only said it a hundred times before—but I shake my head anyway, because that's the game we play.

"Because I loaf you," she says.

"I loaf you too. More than anything." I close my eyes and kiss her.

Get Three E-Books For Free

Building a relationship with my readers is the very best thing about writing. I occasionally send newsletters with details on new releases, special offers and giveaways.

And if you sign up to my mailing list I'll send you all this free stuff:

1. An e-book of *Few Hearts Survive*, a Pink Bean Series novella that is ONLY available to my mailing list subscribers.
2. A free e-book of *Hired Help*, my very first (and therefore very special to me) lesbian erotic romance story.
3. A free e-book of my first 'longer' work, my highly romantic novella *Summer's End*, set on an exotic beach in Thailand.

You can get *Few Hearts Survive* (a Pink Bean Series novella), *Hired Help* (a spicy F/F novelette) and *Summer's End* (a deeply romantic lesfic novella) **for free** by signing up at www.harperbliss.com/freebook/ or scanning the QR code below

About the Author

Harper Bliss is a best-selling lesbian romance author. Among her most-loved books are the highly dramatic French Kissing and the often thought-provoking Pink Bean series.

Harper lived in Hong Kong for seven years, travelled the world for a bit, and has now settled in the Belgian countryside with her wife, Caroline, and her photogenic cat, Dolly Purrton.

Harper loves hearing from readers and you can reach her at the email address below.

www.harperbliss.com
harper@harperbliss.com

Made in United States
Troutdale, OR
01/29/2024

17255181R10159